WILD ATLANTIC WORDS

A COLLECTION OF SHORT STORIES

FROM

MEAS WRITERS

Bunlacky Press

Published by Bunlacky Press
First published in Ireland in 2016 by
Bunlacky Press, Castletown, Dunkineely
County Donegal

ISBN 978-0-9931784-2-9

'Ruby Red Soldiers' was first published in Ruby Red
Cravings, & Strings
'The Bloodstone' was first published in Pheonix Irish Short
Stories 1999 (ed. David Marcus)

Cover design by Kim Pereira
Cover photograph by Dermott Sweeney
Edited by Carolyn Farrar

Sean-Dún na nGall

Is grá geal mo chroí thú, 'Thír Chonaill, a stór,
'Do luí mar bheadh seoid ghlas san fharraige mór,
Ó gráim thú i gcónaí go moch is go mall,
Is molfaidh mé a choích' thú, a Shean-Dún na nGall.

Níl contae in Éirinn níos deise ná thú,
Níl daoine sa domhan níos fearr cáil is clú,
Ná tá i dTír Chonaill abhus agus thall.
Ó! Bláth bán ár dtíre thú, a Shean-Dún na nGall.

Tá teanga ár sinsear á labhairt ann go fóill
Chomh milis binn blasta le hamhrán nó ceol
Na n-aingeal sna Flaithis gan smachtú gan smál,
Ó gráim go deo thú, a Shean-Dún na nGall.
(Carl Hardebeck 1869-1945)

Old Donegal

You are the bright love of my heart, darling country of Conal
Lying as would green silk on the great sea
Oh, I love you always, early and slowly
And I praise you always, ancient Donegal

There is no county in Ireland nicer than you
There are no people in the world of better fame and repute
Nor is there in the country of Conal, in whatever region
Oh, you are the white flower of the land, ancient Donegal.

The tongue of our ancestors is spoken there still
As sweet, pleasant and delicious as song or music
Or angels in Heaven without stain or fault
Oh I love you forever, ancient Donegal.

Acknowledgements

We want to thank all those who supported and encouraged us through the years, particularly the Donegal VEC Adult Education, now Donegal ETB, who facilitated our creative writing courses; the people who attended our public events and all those who helped at various stages.

We also thank those poets and writers who participated over the years.

The Village Teashop in Mountcharles provided the venue for many of our meetings and we thank Lorraine for her support and the Londis Ladies for the photocopying.

We also want to thank all funders, workshop facilitators and those who helped with venues and facilities for our bi-weekly meetings over the years, including local Cllr. John Campbell.

This collection would not have been possible without the guidance and editing skills of Carolyn Farrar and to her we offer our heartfelt thanks.

This book is dedicated to all our people who have left these shores and also to those who have come to us on this island from far and near.

Contents

The Bee's Knees
Malachy Sweeney

A seagull swooped high and dropped a mussel on to the rocks below. He glided to the shore and opened the stunned seashell. Across the bay, the Atlantic swell crashed on to the golden sand. The sound echoed across the water to the little three-roomed cottage at the roadside, where two white chickens roosted on a blue windowsill.

In the living room there was the rhythmic tick of the wall clock and the gentle hum of the kettle on the white Stanley range. Minnie was dozing after dinner and her head lifted slowly when the dog barked. His yelps drew closer and she peered through heavy, brown-rimmed glasses towards the small window and across the road to the sea. The chickens attempted flight as they scurried away amid a mix of their loud cackles and excited yelps from the dog.

'That'll be Packie now,' she murmured.

Johnny sat on the wooden form by the small window, with hands folded on his knee. 'Aye, that'll be

Packie, all right,' he agreed, and adjusted his tweed cap.

With the silence now broken, the canary came to life with a sudden burst of song. Minnie looked towards the cage that hung from the boarded ceiling.

'Will ye listen to that thing,' she said. She was sitting in her usual place in the corner, beside the range. Her feet were planted firmly on the floor and set slightly apart, showing her heavy legs with black stockings. There was something almost defiant about her demeanour, the way she sat like a duchess in her high-backed armchair. Usually she wore a heavy tweed skirt, but in the balmy days of summer she wore a light skirt and a white blouse, and left her black or red cardigan hung on the back of the chair. For almost twenty years she hadn't ventured too far from the chair, ever since she had that 'little episode' on the front street. No one was sure what happened, but she never ventured out again and was tended hand and foot by the rest of the family. Despite this she seemed to thrive, and Johnny was heard to voice the opinion that she would probably outlive the whole lot of them, and even get a cheque from the President.

The dog barked again, the canary pecked at the seed and there was a creaking of floorboards. Johnny looked towards the upper bedroom door as it was pulled open. Grace emerged into the living room, like a moth from some hidden place. She moved quietly across the bare concrete floor, still adjusting her dress.

'I just lay down for a few minutes and must have

dozed off,' she explained.

'It's not surprising. It's sultry, right enough,' Johnny said.

'Aye sultry enough,' Minnie echoed.

The dog gave another excited bark and scraped at the red door. Minnie pursed her lips and said, 'That divil of a dog … he'll soon have that door destroyed, and it's just been painted.'

There was the crunch of boots on the gravel street and a rattle of the latch. With the door half-open, the dog pushed through and came running into the house. He whirled in excitement, before Packie appeared from the porch where he had deposited his dirty wellingtons. 'Will ye sit down, Bran, and get into your bed,' Packie commanded. The dog stood and watched his master make his way to the range. Packie shook the kettle and moved it on to the hot ring. 'My tongue is out for a drop of tea,' he declared.

Grace lifted the teapot. 'Will you ever sit down and rest your legs, sure we'll all have a mouthful,' she said. She was still light on her feet despite her sixty or more years and stood at the sink unit washing cups and humming, "The Homes of Donegal". She still had the heart and spirit of a teenager, despite being two years older than her sister. Her shoulder-length silver hair and patterned dress gave her slim body an elegant appearance, and she insisted that it was her love of the garden and the fresh air that kept her young at heart.

'Did anyone get the weather forecast?' Packie asked.

'No. We missed it on the radio,' Minnie said.

'Sure we'll see it on the television later on.'

'Well damn the bit difference it makes anyway. There'll be no change for a while, as long as the wind is up north-east. It'll be dry enough but cold,' Johnny predicted.

'Sure, they never get it right anyway. You'd be as well off looking out the door yerself,' Packie suggested, with a dismissive shake of his head.

Grace rinsed out the brown, delph teapot and wet the tea. The steaming hot tea was poured into four blue-rimmed mugs. As usual, Minnie dined sitting in her chair while the others sat around the wooden table with the red, patterned tablecloth that matched the glow off the Sacred Heart lamp on the little wooden shelf. Grace cut slices of the homemade scone that she liberally coated with rhubarb jam. Packie was first to savour the rich flavour. 'Man a dear, you can't beat the homemade jam,' he declared, giving a satisfied smack of his lips.

'It's powerful stuff right enough,' Johnny agreed.

The dog stood at Johnny's knee, watching every move and tilting his head. Johnny took another bite and threw the last piece to the dog, who caught it and ran to his bed.

Minnie took a sip of tea and squirmed on the chair before she spoke. 'What was it you were saying about that settee? Didn't you say it was good value and very comfortable?'

'Aye. The one with the two chairs,' Packie

prompted.

Not to be outdone, Johnny said, 'Sure they all have two chairs.'

Grace paused and rested her mug on the table, seemingly pleased that they were all waiting on her to speak. 'I saw it in that second-hand furniture place that's just opened. It's a nice size and it looks very comfortable.'

'And what about the colour? Sure we don't want something too bright,' Minnie said.

'There's no problem there. They have various colours but the one that caught my eye was black.'

'How would black look in here?' Packie asked, glancing around the room.

'Well, at least it wouldn't show the dirt,' Johnny suggested.

Minnie scowled and shuffled her feet on the floor. 'Dirt! Do you hear him?'

There was a lull and Packie enquired, 'And what other colours do they have anyway?'

Grace thought a moment. 'Well, there was a white one and another that was wine-coloured.'

'What about the size?' Johnny asked.

All eyes scanned the room from the sink unit at the back door to the Stanley range at the upper bedroom wall, and to the delph-laden dresser beside the lower bedroom door.

'The settee would fit on the back wall, up from the sink unit,' Grace suggested. She glanced towards Minnie. 'And you could get one of the armchairs.'

Minnie clutched the two arms of the chair, and pushed out her feet, showing the brown leather shoes with a hole cut for her bunion. 'Black you say. And I'd have to get rid of this one.'

'And no harm, either. We can use it to light the fire,' Johnny said with a laugh that faded when Minnie gave him a withering look.

'What about the other chair? Where will it go?' Grace asked.

Minnie looked across at Johnny sitting on the form. 'We'll have to move the form. Maybe we could burn it too,' she said.

Johnny, ignoring the comment, looked around, surveying the space. 'I don't think it would fit in here anyway. It might block the upper bedroom door.'

'And what size is it?' Packie asked.

Grace held out her hands, adjusted them slightly. 'It would be about that width.'

Packie spread his hands to a similar width and checked the space. 'If it's that width, it might be all right. Anyway, sure we'll see how it goes.'

'An' would it be fairly strong?' Minnie asked.

Grace smiled as she recalled the encounter in the shop. 'Funny enough, I asked the man same question.'

'And what did he say?'

'Well, you won't believe this. He took off his shoes, stepped up on the settee and did a little dance. That's what he did. And it didn't take a flinch out of it.'

'Huh. I'm sure we won't be dancing on it,' Minnie said.

Johnny glanced towards Minnie and spoke in a low voice. 'No. I don't suppose she'll do any dancing. And that's for sure.'

Grace pretended not to hear the comment, stifled a smile and held up the delph teapot. 'Does anyone want more tea?'

There were no takers and the conversation drifted to and fro. It was agreed that Grace would call and buy the settee on Friday when she was in town doing the weekly shopping.

***

That was where the matter rested until Saturday, when there was the crunch of tyres on the gravel street and the quiet hum of an engine. The dog barked and ran around the floor.

'Will ye sit down, dog,' Packie growled.

Johnny looked out over the lace curtain. 'That'll be yer man now,' he said.

Grace went to the door and saw a stocky figure opening the rear doors of the van. The man turned and smiled. 'I take it I have the right house. One black settee and two chairs for Grace Doyle.'

He almost sang the last two words. Grace blushed modestly. 'That's me. And we can't wait to see the furniture in the house.'

'We'll you won't have to wait much longer. Now, let's see what we're up against.' He strode forward with a tape in hand. In the porch he hitched up his well-worn corduroy trousers and began to measure. 'This will tell the story,' he mused.

Grace folded her arms and stood watching as he extended the tape and moved into various positions. He stood for a minute as if it might change matters. Then he gave a shake of his head and said, 'As sure as my name is Mick Roper, there's no way it'll fit round that corner.'

At the sound of his voice the dog barked, Minnie shook her head and Packie called, 'Will ye sit down, dog.'

Grace put her hand to her mouth. 'Oh dear me. It won't fit, you say. Then what do we do now?'

'Don't worry. Just you leave it to me. I'll think of something,' Mick assured her.

Packie made his way out to the porch. 'If you need a lift, myself and Johnny can give you a hand,' he suggested.

Mick nodded towards the van. 'That's powerful and I have Flash with me as well. But that's not the problem. It's the turn on the porch. It's just too tight.' Then he paused, had a sudden look of inspiration, and held up one finger. 'What about the back door?'

Packie looked sombre and shook his head. 'Ah now, there could be a problem there. Just you come with me till I show you.' He led the way as they entered the living room. Mick raised a hand in salute, acknowledging Minnie and Johnny. It was like a signal that set the dog off around the room barking.

'Sit down, you brute,' Packie said.

The dog ran towards his bed, hesitated and snapped at Mick's ankle. Mick drew back looking startled.

'Don't mind him. He's harmless,' Johnny said.

The dog settled, and Packie pointed to the back door. 'You see - there's the problem. It would be fine only for the sink unit. We had nowhere else to put it.'

Mick studied the back door that was blocked by the sink unit with the waste pipe disappearing through the door. His deliberations were interrupted by Johnny, who explained, 'Sure we never used to use that oul door anyway.'

'I see … I see,' Mick said slowly, while weighing up the situation. He gave a sudden nod of his head and announced to all, 'If you ask me, there's only one thing for it. Once we get the water turned off we can move the whole shooting gallery in two minutes.'

Mick scanned the room, waiting on a response. Minnie shuffled her feet on the floor before she spoke. 'You say there's nothing else for it.'

'No missus! Nothing else for it, I'm afraid.'

'Sure if there's nothing else for it, then we may give it a shot. We have nothing to lose,' Packie agreed.

'Nothing to lose,' Johnny echoed. 'Nothing at all.'

No time was lost. The water was turned off at the stopcock near the front door and Mick hailed Flash. But there was no response to the call.

'Probably sleeping again,' Mick muttered and roared, 'Flash are you in the land of the living at all. Bring in the bloody tools before it gets dark.'

The van door swung open. A few seconds passed before a denim-clad leg appeared, and then a figure wearing a black beret lurched out of the vehicle. He straightened up, seemingly unsure, and then focused on the front door. One hand clutched a box of tools as he stumbled up the gravel street.

Glances were exchanged, with Grace asking, 'Is he all right?'

Mick shook his head slowly. 'Honestly, missus. I've been asking myself that question for years and your guess is as good as mine.'

'Sure it takes all kinds,' Johnny said.

'You can say that again,' Mick agreed.

No more was said while pipes were loosened, the sink unit moved and the door unscrewed from its hinges. Grace swept behind the sink unit and discovered a bread knife that had disappeared almost a year earlier. She held it up declaring, 'And we thought it was the fairies took it.'

'Huh. Fairies! I'm sure,' Minnie muttered.

While space was cleared inside, Johnny used a slash hook to clear a vigorous growth of briars that encroached outside the back door. Then the men moved to the front street. Grace looked out the window and gave a running commentary to Minnie. 'They have the two armchairs on the street, and now they're easing the settee out of the van. And they're going around the gable now. Goodness gracious me, I just can't wait to see it inside.'

***

Outside, each man took a corner of the settee and they shuffled along towards the gable. A few hens were hushed out of the way near the back door. Mick gave an occasional command: 'Steady on now, boys. We're almost there. Mind the step now. Leave her down there and we'll take a breather.'

'Thank Christ,' Johnny murmured softly.

When the settee was lifted once more there was a shuffling of feet to line up for the door. The dog got excited again and snapped at Flash's extended leg. Flash swung his heel and roared, 'Clear away to blazes, dog.'

'He'll do no harm. He's a big pet,' Johnny assured him, but Flash was not impressed.

'Pet or not, he'll get a hard toe up the ass if he comes near me again.'

Packie roared, 'Get away to hell dog, and into your bed.'

Mick kept his mind on the work. 'Steady on now boys,' he cautioned. 'Tilt her up at an angle, and mind the hands on the door frame. A wee bit higher, men.'

'She's looking good,' Johnny said with a satisfied sigh when the settee slipped through the doorway. It only took a few more heaves and groans before the settee was set down, and the two armchairs were sitting on the floor minutes later. Even then, no time was lost admiring the new furniture. Flash and Johnny held the back door steady while Mick secured the hinges.

***

It was only when the sink unit was back in position, with the waste pipe out through the door, that attention was turned to the layout of the new furniture. The old form and Minnie's chair were shipped off to the shed while the settee and chairs were organised: 'Move it a bit this way,' 'Just angle it slightly,' 'No, no, a bit too much,' and so on, until there was broad agreement.

Without hesitation, Johnny made the first move. He sat on the chair beside the window and raised his two legs playfully in the air. 'I declare to God you wouldn't know the place. It's the bee's knees,' he said.

Grace sat gingerly on the settee, and then relaxed with a broad smile. Packie waited, looking at the others to gauge their reaction.

'Will ye sit down and relax,' Grace insisted, and patted the settee invitingly

Packie pointed to his old grime-coated boiler suit. 'No. I think I'll wait until I have my middling good trousers on.'

Strangely enough, there was no comment from Minnie, who seemed to have sunk into the upholstery and had somehow lost her air of authority. Grace sensed that the silence was ominous and said, 'Your seat looks very comfortable, Minnie.'

Minnie's hands grasped at the armrests and her

feet slipped on the floor as she struggled to sit up. It took a moment before she responded. 'Aye. But I'm not gone on the colour. The whole room looks a bit too dark, don't you think?'

Grace had her mouth half-open to respond when Minnie continued. 'Maybe we should have gone for another colour. I'm not sure about the black.' And she wasn't finished yet, adding in a louder voice, 'An' as well - I liked my oul chair better.'

There was a moment's silence, maybe even two. Johnny threw his eyes to heaven. Packie whistled a nervous nothing. Grace brushed her hand along the settee. Flash moved his weight nervously from one leg to the other.

Mick lifted the toolbox and edged towards the door. He glanced at the back door and the sink unit, and then nodded towards the settee. 'If you're thinking of taking it out again, you could always cut it in half and it would come out the front door handy enough.'

With that he was out the door with Flash at his heels, and showing an unexpected burst of speed. The silence was broken by Mick Roper's voice, which came drifting back through the open doorway: 'Good luck now.'

You could have heard a pin drop in the house. Even the dog seemed caught by surprise.

'You didn't offer them tea,' Grace said.

'Huh! Tea, I'm sure,' Minnie muttered.

'I think they were in a hurry,' Johnny suggested.

'We'll get used ...'

The van doors banged and the engine growled into life. There was a sudden spinning of wheels with loose gravel flying. The dog tore out through the doorway and raced after the van. The vehicle gathered speed and splashed through a large, muddy pothole, sending a shower of spray over the dog. He came to a standstill, stood for a second, turned and ran into the house. Minnie glared at the wet animal. 'Will you look at the cut of that thing,' she said.

The words were barely out of her mouth when the dog gave an almighty shake of its body and sent a shower of spray across the room and over Minnie's white blouse. The droplets hissed on the hot range, but it wasn't near as loud as Minnie's hiss, 'You DIRTY divil of a dog.'

Bran seemed to sense the tone of her voice. He ran and brushed along the settee as he retreated to a safer place, under the table. Johnny eyed the dirty, wet streak on the settee. 'If you ask me...I think we were lucky we didn't go for the white one,' he observed.

Packie looked at the wet splotches on his boiler suit and thought, *It's a bloody good job that I didn't have my middling good trousers on, they'd have been ruined for sure.*

The kettle began to sing on the range and Grace, who was humming, "The Old Bog Road," rose to her feet.

'I think, after all that excitement, we deserve a nice cup of hot tea,' she suggested.

There were welcome murmurs of agreement

from everyone.

***

Outside, the two white chickens peered cautiously from under the hedge and then reclaimed their roost on the blue windowsill. A heron stood patiently at the water's edge. In the distance the swell rolled in from the broad Atlantic and crashed on to the sandy beach, but all was quiet once more at the little three-roomed cottage by the sea.

Dark Heart
Marie Hannigan

St John's Eve: two days past the June solstice, the latest hour of sunset in Donegal. And tonight, all going to plan, Roseanne will cross paths with a murderer. On this final night of the Midsummer Festival it's party time in the village. To the passengers from the cruise liner it must seem as if the entire population has come out to meet them.

Not quite all.

Roseanne and her companions have witnessed the celebrations from the shrine above the town. They are on the hunt for a miracle. Caught in the banter between Jade and pensioner, Peggy, it occurs to Roseanne that they represent the three stages of womanhood.

Dusk has fallen since they climbed to the well from the car park at the end of the new road where Jodie's friend, Breen, had dropped them off. For the miracle to work they would have to take the old way back, the dark way. Roseanne is anxious, as much afraid of failure as of apprehending the fearsome McDowell.

Breen had wished them luck before turning the orange minibus and heading back for the village. There'd be music in the Diamond, and things always got a bit crazy once the drink took hold. Breen has volunteered to pick up the casualties and deliver them safely back to home or ship.

***

The beat of a rock band rises from the village. Below, in the curve of harbour, the town fades into the glow of festive bulbs usually reserved for the other end of the year. The festival is bigger than ever this year, a "Mardi Gras" put on for the cruise passengers. In this way Christmas and Lent have merged with the old tradition of Bonfire Night. Since the local ban on outdoor burning, the festival weekend has replaced an evening that once flared and crackled with the tang of burning wood.

Way back in Peggy's youth they danced around the bonfire to accordion music. Even Jade is not too young to remember a time when mighty hillocks of rubber tyres were torched.

On such an evening Roseanne had met her future on Rossnowlagh beach. She recalled the cheers as sparks burst above their heads, the way the blaze flickered in his eyes. They'd fed the fire far into the night. At the first streaks of dawn he'd grabbed her hand and they leaped the dying embers together. Love at first sight, they called it.

Five sons in eight years. Enough, he said, enough of a family for any man to carry. He had a point, but Roseanne wanted a girl. She was thirty when Sona was born and she named her daughter for the joy of that moment. Aisling, her dream child, was the unexpected bonus. An infant on her knee, a noisy rabble around the dinner table, those years Roseanne remembers as her happiest.

'Don't take it personally, Mum,' Aisling had said, when Sona set off on the backpacking trail. 'Everyone goes travelling. I'll be heading away too when I'm her age.'

But Aisling doesn't know the full story.

***

Before Roseanne set out from the house, she sent another email to Sona. There will be a reply by the time she gets home, or so she tells herself.

They walk the stations in twilight, the best time for a miracle according to Peggy. She explains the ritual, the prayers, the slow circling of the well. She comes here regularly, for the good of her soul. 'You need shag-all else at my time of life,' she says. Jade doesn't believe in miracles. She does the stations with them anyway. Her intention, Roseanne suspects, is the same dream everybody holds, were you to look beneath the Facebook smiles.

The sun slips behind Crownarad. On the hills beyond the town the flare of renegade bonfires becomes visible. Smoke billows into the sky to merge with the rain clouds massing against the sunset afterglow.

While the women wait the hour before full dark they sit smoking, chatting about the events of the day, events that have brought them to the shrine tonight.

This is Roseanne's search, really. Peggy is here out of stubbornness and Jade has come along as their bodyguard. It's not safe, she maintains, for two old dolls to be wandering about on the final night of the festival.

***

That afternoon, in the dappled sunlight of the ancient graveyard, Peggy had scoffed at the notion. 'Are you feared some scallywag would steal our honour? That ship has long since sailed, a grá.'

They had been basking in the shelter of the churchyard walls, a haven of wild flowers and humming insects. To the librarian, their supervisor, the churchyard was a place that nurtured biodiversity and for added bonus, a heritage site. For Setanta's team it was a break from the routine of researching yellowed manuscripts. A bunch of women from seventeen to seventy, they'd behaved like children let out of school for the afternoon. On the first day a man had turned up. One look at Jade's scalped head, and he'd reversed out the door, never to return. There were volunteers from the Historical Society, ladies with formidable knowledge of parish records. And there was Peggy who carried the saltier oral version. Roseanne and the others had been put on the scheme for want of alternative employment, yet it's hard to resist the librarian's passion for the history project.

Today's task had been to match the characters in the library manuscripts with the names carved into the tilting tombstones which were, according to Setanta, the oldest and most reliable written history of the parish. Peggy was jotting down the names and dates, or as much as Jade's keen eyes could decipher, while the others cleared a narrow path around the overgrown graves. Setanta had armed them with grass clippers and a warning to cut only the dying sedge, leaving tufts here and there of still flowering plants.

They'd have used nail scissors if he asked. The young ones are half in love with the handsome librarian. Even the more mature - who can appreciate beauty without wishing to get entangled with it - would do anything to bring a smile to the Christ-like features.

From time to time the supervisor gifted them with a nod of approval. This morning they'd seen full-blooded joy on that gorgeous face. He'd come into the library with a jaunt in his step, having the night before proposed to the love of his life at the peak of Sliabh Liag where he'd brought her for the occasion.

After she'd thrown her arms about his neck

they'd made passionate, hours-long, love.

The last bit he didn't reveal, but what else would you do, Peggy insisted, when you've nabbed the finest shift in the parish? Rough laughter merged with the sound of birdsong that filled the grounds of the abandoned church. At the best of times, Peggy is crude and raucous; her sixty-a-day cackle every bit as infectious as Setanta's enthusiasm.

The pensioner is the one who flirts with their supervisor. The two younger ones come into the library every morning dressed and made up for a night on the town. Setanta is bombarded with endless questions – anything for notice.

Jade doesn't resort to such strategies. She is strong girl, not easily bent to anybody's rule. She challenges Setanta at every opportunity. Yet the shaven-headed doll who had arrived the first day, announcing that she'd be out of there as soon as she got a half-assed job, that same girl is the most conscientious of all. More telling, Jade has allowed the stubble to grow out to a spiky halo.

Setanta is oblivious. To him she is the troublemaker. He is young, as yet untutored in the tangled ways of negative attention-seeking. He does not see the pretty face beneath the hedgehog hairdo. And Jade is pretty, beautiful actually. On a rare night out with Peggy, Roseanne had seen the young woman, eyes kohl-lined like an Egyptian queen, traipsing after some lads, impatient types who hustled the girl away when she stopped to pass a few words with her workmates.

'At the beck and call of every bowsie,' Peggy had muttered. 'That girl has no notion of her own worth.'

The crush on Setanta, while hopeless, was fixed at least on a worthy object.

And there is Breen, the neighbour lad who drops Jade off at the library every morning, and who pulls in to give her co-workers a lift. Beauty and the Beast, Peggy calls them. Breen is a big lad, with bulk to match his height. And while he is not as handsome as some, there is good nature in his eyes and adoration when he sets those eyes on Jade.

According to Peggy, young ones don't appreciate *nice*. The looks and the thrills fade soon enough. Love is as love does, she wheezes. You could tell them all that. And you'd be wasting your breath. Didn't we all chase the bad boys, the nice-looking ones with the snaky hips? Ah Peggy we did, her workmates agree.

Setanta is as decent a bloke as you could find, but he carries the irresistible glamour of the unobtainable.

He was at the farthest corner of the graveyard carefully trimming a blackberry briar as Peggy's voice rose, describing in detail what she would do if she ever got her hands on their young supervisor.

Roseanne took on a coughing fit for fear he might catch an inkling of the object of the women's amusement.

'What's the joke?' Smiling, Setanta picked his way towards them.

'Catch it while it's flying.' Peggy pulled out her

selfie stick. 'We're taking a snap, come on in and join us.'

It was while stepping back to include him in the photograph that she literally stumbled across McDowell's grave. Cursing, she lowered herself to the grass, picked up the clump of moss she'd dislodged - and spied what had lain concealed beneath it. The corner edge of a slab stone. Peggy ran her fingers along the rim.

'Peggy, be careful,' Setanta warned. Too late. Peggy was not for stopping till she'd uncovered the details carved into the fallen tombstone.

Here lieth the body of
Alexander Henry McDowell
who departed this life
May the 18th 1846 aged 38 years

Beneath the inscription, a less formal hand had gouged an epithet: *The Dark Heart*. There were other words scraped into the stone, graffiti that described the hateful nature of the deceased.

'Well?' Peggy folded her arms across her chest. 'Is that enough proof for you?'

Setanta's frown had transformed to elation. Of all the characters who had come up in their research McDowell had been the most contentious. Up to this point, the librarian had been convinced that Dark Heart was a generic name for the oppressor, the archetypal villain where all the old stories merged. No one man, he'd suggested, was capable of the wickedness attributed to Alexander McDowell: evictions, murders; a pregnant scullery maid thrown from the window of the master's bedroom. McDowell was so wicked, they said, that the hounds of hell bayed the night he died and Evil itself came to claim him – body and soul.

Yet here he was, sleeping beneath his mossy blanket, the Dark Heart himself.

Setanta's happiest day was complete. He paced the ground, measuring out the exact location on his map of the graveyard. When they'd entered the details in the book of souls, he lifted the spongy rug and replaced it carefully over the grave.

***

On their return to the library, they'd broken out a jumbo pack of chocolate biscuits to celebrate. In the months of research, Dark Heart was the character who'd captured their interest. He stalked across the pages, his wickedness more vivid than any of the dry details of local bigwigs. But only one written account connected Dark Heart to the landlord; the newspaper report of an incident in the parish.

The slope that separated the church from the shrine formed part of McDowell's extensive property. Throughout the hungry 1840s, the path to the well was thronged with the dispossessed in search of an answer to their prayers. Infuriated by the hordes crossing his land, McDowell bricked up the path to the holy well and set his hounds on the few with the strength to scale the wall. Soon after, his house was flooded by a spout of water that erupted through the kitchen floor. Not until the path was reopened did the water subside.

That year the herring shoaled so close to the shore it was possible to wade into the water and gather them in the creel baskets used for carrying turf.

McDowell was dead before the season was out. Another miracle.

Setanta had dismissed the report as sensationalism. Every storyteller put their own spin on a yarn, and writers were the worst liars. 'Never let the truth stand in the way of a good story, that's their motto,' he said.

While the others munched their chocolate bickies, Peggy was rooting through the files. She shook the cutting in Setanta's face.

'Now can we put it in our history of the parish?'

Setanta brushed the crumbs from his beard. 'When was the last time you heard of a miracle, Peggy?'

He had a point. Such extraordinary events were seldom reported in recent times. Peggy had a theory about that. Death had not deterred McDowell from harassing pilgrims: An encounter with his ghost on the lane from the well was the penance you paid for an answer to your prayer. But no one used the haunted path now, not since the new road gave easy access to the shrine.

'If you're right, and McDowell is part of the miracle, maybe he's trying to redeem his sins.' Setanta smiled. He was teasing and Peggy knew it.

'Right,' she said. 'Come to the well with me the night and I'll prove it 'till ye.'

Only one person had accepted Peggy's challenge. Roseanne was as sceptical as the supervisor, but she needed a miracle. What was there to lose?

***

They've all but reached the end of the path that runs along the walls of the church. The stalks of streetlights are visible just ahead. Peggy crosses herself.

'Thanks be to God we have that behind us.'

They should have met McDowell along the way. There's neither sight nor sound of him and Roseanne has gone queasy with disappointment. 'Where is he?'

Jade squints into the dusk. 'Guess he's a no-show.'

'Naw, he's snoking about alright.' The old woman's breath is coming hard.

'Sure enough,' Jade says, 'the hair is standing on me.'

Roseanne rubs her goose-bumped arms, wishing she'd brought a cardigan. 'It always seems chilly when the sun goes down, especially after a warm day like today.' If facing McDowell is the price of the miracle, she has to find him. 'There's only one place he can be,' she says.

Their heads swivel towards the churchyard.

'Ah no,' Peggy pleads, 'we've done enough. Let us head away before the rain comes on.'

'You've been brilliant, both of you. Go on home ye now. I'm not afraid to face him on my own.' Roseanne turns onto the path to the churchyard. The gates are rusted closed. She will get inside as they did this morning. She has her first step on the stile by the time the others catch up with her. Peggy claws her arm.

'You're not going in there in the pitch-black night?'

'I'll be grand.' Roseanne pats Peggy's hand and pulls free. She climbs to the top of the stile. 'Come on, Dark Heart,' she shouts into the pit below. 'Face me now - if you ever existed.'

'In the name of all that's holy, don't invoke that devil,' Peggy wails. 'Pull her down out of there, Jade, for I'm not fit.'

Before the girl has time to reach her, Roseanne skitters down the steps into the churchyard.

Here the cloak of trees obscures what remains of grey light. In the blinding darkness all that can be seen is the looming ruin. Roseanne tries to remember the location of the grave. Wasn't it somewhere behind the church? She picks her way over the lumpy ground, pushing through briars and nettles. Her foot catches on the lip of a tomb and she sprawls onto her knees. The gravestone is too solid to be McDowell's. She rears to her feet.

'Where are you, you bastard?'

Suddenly, Jade is by her side. She links Roseanne's arm and huddles close. 'He's here, all around us. Can you not feel him, Roseanne?'

Roseanne feels only disappointment, for if there is no McDowell, neither is there a miracle.

Her lovely Sona, her beloved child, will continue to block all attempts to make amends.

Through this long evening the storm clouds have gathered. Now it starts, a deluge cracking against the oak leaves. She turns to the shivering girl. 'I can't see the grave. Will you help me find it?'

Jade whips out her mobile phone. 'Time to call in reinforcements,' she says.

Dearest child, Roseanne had written in the email to Sona. *My heart hurts. Please, before this night is out, please get back to me.*

Tonight she'd packed away Aisling's school uniform for the final time and watched her youngest getting dolled up to celebrate. In the chaos of raising seven children, Roseanne could never have imagined the moment when all but one would be off to foreign parts, when that baby, would be set to leave for college. 'They're reared now,' their father announced one night. 'I've done my bit.'

***

The beam of a torch appears: Breen on the night's first rescue mission. Jade calls out to guide him and as the light wobbles closer she takes a running jump into his arms and wraps slender legs around his waist. 'Beast, I love you,' she says. So she should, Roseanne thinks. Any fellow staunch enough to leave the town party and brave the haunted graveyard, that lad deserves all good things.

Breen shines the torchlight on a mossy space between gravestones.

'Yeah, I'm sure that's the place,' Jade says.

Roseanne can't tell if this is McDowell's grave. She can see no shadowy form. No voice whispers foul words in her ear, no icy hand reaches out to clutch her breast. But she can hear Peggy's voice, urging them to hurry, for she is perished with the cold.

***

It is almost midnight by the time Roseanne gets home. The computer is still running. Messages swirl in, ads for all manner of offers. Not a word from Sona.

When their father decided to go his own way, there'd been a flurry of Skype calls from the boys. They were sympathetic but unsurprised.

Sona had blamed her mother. It was too much to bear. And Roseanne reacted in the worst possible way. Those bitter words were the last spoken between them before Sona stepped on a plane to Thailand. Since then, unanswered texts, unanswered emails.

'Just call her, Mom,' Aisling has said a million times. 'It's free when you use the app.'

But that would invite direct rejection. And Sona might be sleeping still. All those different time zones, Roseanne can never get them right.

If I wake her will it be another black mark against me?

So be it, she thinks. Nothing could be worse than this agony.

Sona answers on the first ring. 'Mom?'

'Yes, it's me.' Roseanne waits interminable moments for the ring-off tone.

When Sona finally speaks, her words come in hiccups. It's six in the morning in a place called Phuket and she's been sick with fright since an incident in the all-night marketplace.

'I was standing at this food stall waiting to be served. And, Mom, I found your face in crowd. You were walking towards me in that orange dress, the one we bought you for your fiftieth. And I kept staring and staring, wondering how ...? And then you were right up next to me and ... and I saw it was only a Buddhist nun. And I tried to reach home. And Aisling just kept ignoring my calls ... like there'd been some emergency. I was full sure something terrible had happened.'

'It's Bonfire Night,' Roseanne tells her. She doesn't need to explain the deafening music, the fireworks, the rush to a crowded bar to top off the night's entertainment.

'Wish I was there,' Sona says. 'I miss you all.'

There is an awkwardness then, before the words that Roseanne has found so hard to utter come rushing from her throat. In the time lag between them, she hears her daughter's choked apology clashing with the echo of her own.

They will talk into the night, as they always did. And when Aisling comes home, a little tipsy, they will talk and laugh and cry some more.

Peggy would call it a miracle. But that orange dress, Roseanne never wore it. Orange has never been her colour. It doesn't matter. On this night of midsummer it doesn't matter at all.

Little Italy
Clarrie Pringle

Do I remember that day? Do I what? How could I ever forget? Sure don't I relive it in me dreams, that and the day I left my Donegal home for the U.S. of A will be etched in me mind forever, aye.

***

I was walking down the street in Little Italy one Saturday afternoon, dreaming of the Dublin Liberties that the narrow streets and small houses brought to mind, when the thump-thump of brass instruments permeated my consciousness and shocked me back to reality. I stood still, looked back up the street and, Jesus! Was it a Corpus Christi procession or what?

The brass band, bedecked in blue and gold, tassels and ribbons, sashes and fancy hats, with pasta-filled bellies bulging under the weight of instruments, pushed all thoughts of Corpus Christi away. They drew closer while the crowds danced behind them, escorted by NY cops.

There was a huge statue on a sedan-type pole thing, carried by strutting, swarthy little men. Was it St. Joseph? Anthony? Or who? Had to be an Italian fellow, but I couldn't remember the names of any Italian saints. Sure, don't all Italian men think they're gods, anyway? The sad face of the graven image was surrounded by dollar bills sticking out of its ears, nose, hands – everywhere possible.

I joined the parade, couldn't resist it. After all, money, Catholicism and curiosity were universal. We slowly and tunefully made our way down the street.

Suddenly, the musicians stopped and dead-marched in place, the dancing ceased; a roll of drums before silence descended outside a neat little house with an apartment-to-rent sign. Jesus, this was New York, wasn't it?

Was the saint coming to pay his deposit, I wondered. But no, he stayed where he was and a few men in suits gathered round the door – politicians, by the looks of them. Oh yes, definitely politicians. They were the same the world over, pugnacious, portly and polished. Their words were probably the same as well, though delivered in tones different to our wild Atlantic way.

Whatever they were saying it appeared to meet with the approval of the dancers and the band. I couldn't make it out; my ears were still tuned to the other side of the ocean.

They all clapped enthusiastically, some stamping their feet. So it was a rally of some sort, and not, as I had thought, the saint coming with his deposit on the apartment.

I lost interest and continued my sojourn through Little Italy, feeling a bit like a virginal Leopold Bloom. Mind, the virginal state was not elective, just hard luck. I lived in hope, though. A fine big fella like me, able to do the blarney when needed. Amazing the way some of the American women fell for it. Pity was, they were the kind I didn't fancy. Always wanted what I couldn't have. Someday, though, it might happen. Not quite past it yet. Well, hoped I wasn't.

Humming quietly to myself I walked the streets of New York, heading for the centre of all entertainment – intellectual, physical and musical – Washington Square Park. Memories of my first time in the park were still vivid. I thought I had stumbled on to a movie set. Acrobats tumbling competitively around the place, barbershop quartets, operatic arias delivered by full-bosomed women sitting on the grass or draped round a tree, and shock of shocks, a trio of very attractive women dancers who, on closer inspection, turned out to be men dressed as women. In those days I had never heard tell of transvestites. New York really impressed me, a true learning experience.

The April warmth was pleasant as I ambled along, dodging the always hurrying native New Yorkers. Canal Street was alive with the three-card trick men, and some of what I would call thimble men. I stopped to watch a big thimble man – hands doing a ballet of hiding the pea, and the punters doing a death dance of throwing bills on the table and shouting excitedly, 'under that one, that one there', whereupon the dancing hands would lift the three covers slowly. Inevitably, the dance was followed not by applause, but by the punters' sighing, 'uhhhhh' in disappointment, as their dollars disappeared up Thimble's sleeve.

This was fascinating. How could the gamblers be so wrong? How could they miss where the pea was? I watched the dancing hands without blinking and was right every time. Mind, when I started shouting third, middle or whatever, dancing hands stumbled a few times before telling me to 'bug off, man', and the stupid punters wouldn't even listen to me! Oh, well, their loss, and boy, did they lose. Hundreds in minutes gone. I was a 'cute hoor' of an Irishman, not long enough off the boat, and sauntered on, ignoring temptation. My dollars were hard-earned on construction sites round the city. I had a goal to reach before returning to the Emerald Isle to buy my wee farm. I was not going to be deflected by the lure of easy money, no, sir.

***

The park beckoned, and tiring of the pavements, a seat was welcome. I sat under a tree close to where four old men were playing chess. They played silently, with concentration as thick as the cigarette smoke; shaking, gnarled hands made the occasional move. A jazz singer was in full flight a few yards away, and a small audience gathered. Over near the gate a quartet of tenors belted out show tunes to compete for attention. Pleasant and relaxing. I wondered why the park wasn't crowded all the time, there was such a variety going on. But this city had so many attractions.

The chess players had my attention and I didn't raise my eyes immediately. But when I did, I noticed the woman sitting on the bench close by, head back to catch the sun, eyes closed and a little smile on her lips. Her hands were folded on her lap and a feeling of peace emanated from her. I felt something click inside my head before I turned back to the chess men, her image still burning behind my eyes. I could no longer follow the game. For once, I was nervous and unsure. Bothered. Not like myself at all.

How could I make contact? Because I knew I had to. Inwardly flustered and unsure, I rose and ambled over to her, slowly sat on the far end of the bench, keeping my eyes on the chess players, breathing steady enough now. We sat that way, carefully ignoring each other for perhaps five minutes before the woman stirred a little, opened her eyes and turned her head in my direction.

'Hello there.' She smiled.

'Hello,' I answered. 'I hope I didn't disturb your rest.'

'No, not at all,' she said, her Donegal accent now evident. 'You're grand. I saw you earlier and was actually thinking about you. There was something familiar about you.'

'Really? Strange, I thought I recognised you, too.'

She laughed softly. 'Maybe we are kindred spirits … or met in a past life … or something.'

'It's possible,' I agreed. 'It must have been a past life because if it was in this one I wouldn't have let you go.'

With a smile she said, 'Well, let's introduce ourselves and see where we go now. I'm Mary McGinley from the Rosses, and you, you're from west Donegal too. I know by your voice. Is it Glen?'

So that's how it started, in Washington Square Park on an April day. We sat on the bench talking for hours – didn't notice the chess men leaving, the entertainers quietening. And sure what else could we do but walk back up to Little Italy and share a meal, easy in ourselves as though we had been together all our lives.

*****

We learned a lot from our talk that afternoon. Both of us a short enough time in the Big Apple, still feeling transient and unmoored from our roots, but enjoying the experience. Temporary dislocation, we agreed. We had lots in common … music, books and poetry, and after much talk, a sharing of our mutual aspiration of being writers.

Turned out we both lived in Astoria – to us Atlantic Irish a really exotic area, with Steinway Street at its heart – and we were both regulars in Socrates

Sculpture Park down beside the projects. The park had been a city dump until a few years back when the locals took it over and claimed it for their own. It was now the site of all kinds of art – sculpture, rope work, paintings and even music. The music was a series of bells intertwined in a row of trees on the edge of the East River. The melody depended on the strength of the breeze, mainly gentle in the summer but rising to a crescendo in the winter winds.

***

I wondered out loud that we had not run into each other on Steinway or in the park until Mary surprised me, saying 'Well, we did, you know…'

'What? We did what?'

'Run into each other, literally,' she said, and laughed.

'When I opened my eyes in Washington Square today and saw you, I felt I had known you all my life, and wondered why. Then I recalled I had seen you before, in Socrates. Do you remember? One day last month you were standing on the edge of the river looking over at Gracie Mansion, oblivious to everything. I was on the path behind you when the kids kicked a ball that hit you in the back and you nearly fell into the river. I grabbed you just in time and pulled you back. You didn't even blink or say anything. I did the Good Samaritan bit and walked on my way.'

I was shocked. I did remember! It was one of those days when dark thoughts and loneliness of exile crushed the spirit, and the pain of living was nearly too much to bear. The ball had knocked me into the reality of my surroundings! I had barely noticed the woman who had pulled me back … but then I must have subconsciously registered her, else how could I have felt that shock of connection when I saw her in the park?

****

That afternoon with Mary McGinley confirmed the signal of that click in my head: She was, in every sense, 'it' … and not to be lost. Mary never quite told me what her feelings that day had been, save to say that when she felt my presence on the bench beside her, every nerve tensed. When she opened her eyes there was a sense of knowing, and not knowing, with also a feeling of arrival or 'completeness'.

Well, in the ensuing years I have come to know what Mary means when she talks without words, which is most of the time. I know, for her eyes are never silent. I make up for her in that respect – particularly when we are on our annual pilgrimage from Donegal's wild west to Washington Square, and I insist on telling the chess men, the entertainers and anyone who will listen, how I met the love of my life sitting on a bench there one April day.

Of Vegetables and Men
Charlie Garratt

It's dark and damp outside, the coldest night of the year by far, so the air in the smokers' passage is thick with smog not seen since the yard door was last closed against the weather six months earlier. Customers passing through on their way to the gents' or ladies' gasp for breath when the smoke clogs their lungs.

Inside the bar it is warm, and a group of musicians crowd round a table covered with half-full glasses and the paraphernalia of the guitarists and fiddlers. Other than the music makers there are few customers, for it is winter and most of the tourists have disappeared. On the table next to the players there are four men in their twenties, three of a local family. The other is a good-looking American, the cousin backpacking his way across Europe and stopping off in this south-western corner of Donegal to connect with his roots.

An accordionist begins a reel and it's clear that the tune's not well known, as the other players don't join him in the opening notes. Then a fiddler slowly picks up the melody. A bodhrán starts to tap out the emerging rhythm, adding weight to the growing momentum of the music. At last the guitars, bringing further percussive effect, pull in all the remaining fiddlers, accordionists and even a lone uilleann piper until the reel is swirling around the bar in controlled frenzy, layer upon layer of harmony and counterpoint bringing all under its spell, everyone tapping their feet and wearing broad smiles at the spectacle of it.

The door swings open and a slight figure pushes backwards into the bar, struggling to lift a large instrument behind her. Safely inside, the young woman throws back her hood, showing off her shoulder-length black hair, and is recognised by her friend, Patricia, heading to the counter for a refill. The two start to chat, laughing and catching up, before being interrupted by the American who offers to carry the harp to the musician's table. She accepts and gifts him a smile that would send any male weak at the knees.

At the bar sit two men, their conversation interrupted to watch this drama unfold. Pádraig is over seventy; Tom is reaching his thirties and regretting missing his chance to become acquainted with the female newcomer. They have been talking of carrots. Earlier, they'd spoken of the state of the country and the uselessness of politicians to help the west of Ireland.

'Only thing we ever get here first is the rain,' the

older man had said and Tom agreed.

Then their discussion had been on Guinness and the relative merits of normal and extra cold. Both agreed that what is now classified as normal is too damn cold anyway, developed for city-dwelling lager drinkers, whilst the 'extra' would give you a bad stomach. This conversation had not dulled the appetites of either for the black stuff, mutually agreeing to try it 'one more time' to see if it improved. They progressed with these same words most evenings and rarely came to a definite conclusion, having to return the next night to continue their research.

But now the talk had turned to vegetables: how to grow them and, best of all, how their mothers cooked them. Each man spoke with nostalgia, and though Pádraig's mother was long dead and Tom's 'mammy' was young enough to be Pádraig's daughter, this difference didn't seem to bother the two men. Naturally enough their first port of call had been the humble potato, 'Erin's ruin', as Pádraig liked to call it. A casual observer might note the beauty of conversation between them, where a vegetable prompted discourse on subjects as diverse as cookery, horticulture and nineteenth-century politics. Both men agreed that it had been a bad year for the spud; springtime's near-drought and a wet summer had brought the blight and crops had been poor. Tom joked that he'd planted eight pounds of seed and harvested six pounds of potatoes. He was pleased that the older man laughed loudly at this confession.

As a hornpipe bounced along in the corner they'd moved seamlessly on to swedes, the other staple food crop in past times, and Pádraig had bemoaned the loss of the growing of them for the cattle. Tom recounted how, the previous winter, he'd visited northern France and seen piles of swedes in the corner of fields and had been told they were to be used as animal feed. This inevitably led to talk of the Common Agricultural Policy and how French farmers were still able to use traditional methods whilst the Irish and British were forced into greater and greater concentration on economic forms of food production. When their ritual slagging off of the French had been exhausted, Tom and Pádraig agreed that mashed swede, with the addition of buttermilk, was amongst the greatest vegetable dishes on the planet. This, with no premonition of the rocky waters ahead, took them to carrots.

It all began well enough, with Pádraig explaining that there were just three main things to remember when growing them.

'Make sure that the soil is free of stones, else they'll split as they grow. Remember to thin them out. Don't be lazy about it or you'll just end up with loads of small carrots, which are a bugger to peel – though they taste sweet enough. And try to plant onions between the rows to keep away the fly.'

Tom nods sagely, though his mind is wandering to the harpist. Pádraig's words had brought to mind a girl at school, her hair so bright she was christened

"Carrots", and Tom muses on an appropriate simile for the musician's locks. *As black as ink, like the marble stones in Kilkenny*, he thinks, reminded by the last singer's rendition of "Carrickfurgus". *Aye, that's the one.*

Pádraig stops speaking and Tom realises he's been in another place. Taking seriously his responsibility for maintaining the craic, he asks his companion how he likes his carrots cooked. Pádraig says his mother's preference had been for peeling, chopping and long boiling, adding butter after the vegetables had been drained. Tom, who we need to remember had been to France after all, and had been given a Jamie Oliver cookbook for Christmas which had taken him to new heights in the cooking of carrots, uses herbs, spices and white wine.

He voices both his disagreement and his preferred recipe, adding, 'Al dente, that's how they should be.'

'Al Dente? Didn't he used to sing with Dean Martin?' Pádraig laughs.

'You muppet. It's Italian, means crunchy.' Tom ignores the fact that Pádraig's 'dente' had departed many years before.

'Rubbish, nothing like soft, sweet carrots soaking in butter.'

Tom, now with something to prove, pulls another customer and the landlord into the conversation.

'Which would you prefer?' he asks. 'Sloppy,

greasy carrots or lightly cooked ones gently broiled in cumin, parsley and white wine?'

This, far from resolving the matter, only serves to fan the flames, as the third man at the bar was of Pádraig's generation, had lived with his mother for more years than was good for either of them, and favoured over-boiling. The landlord, on the other hand, had been in the hotel trade for most of his working life, regularly took foreign holidays and fancies himself as something of a *bon viveur*. All had known each other long enough that they were not predisposed to guard their words and a furious row ensues, with so much din that the musicians lay down their instruments. Some go for a smoke, and others carry on their own slant on the discussion, each side shouting taunts, with much hilarity, at the main combatants at the bar.

During a communal pause for breath, a still, clear note splits the silence. Soon a lament, sung in the Irish, rises and falls, telling of deepest ardour and a broken heart. Everyone can feel this, whether they have the language or not. All remain quiet and as the young woman's voice fills the room, sweet and melodious as the harp she plays, each man there knows that he is in love.

With the battle now forgotten, a single tear trickles down Pádraig's cheek and Tom can't take his eyes from the singer.

***

'Saoirse, isn't it?'

'It is. Do I know you?'

'I don't think so. I'm a cousin of Patricia Gallagher.' Tom had seized his chance when he spotted the American head out with the other smokers. All night he'd had to sit and watch his rival throwing compliments and Saoirse gladly catching them. Now it was Tom's turn and he grabs a seat beside her at the musicians' table.

'Loved the song, by the way.'

'Thanks. Do you sing yourself?'

He shakes his head. 'No 'fraid not. At least not like you, anyway. Can I get you a drink?'

Saoirse says he needn't bother but lets him bring her a glass of sparkling water when he insists. She watches Tom blush when an older man walking by whispers in his ear and laughs, glancing in her direction as he does so.

They chat as best they can between the tunes, he telling her he's a carpenter and trying to learn the guitar, she telling him she's a music teacher in Dublin, just home for a few days. The American now sees his cause is lost and returns to talk to his cousins. Tom knows most of the men in the session and several give him a knowing wink whenever Saoirse sings and plays, and although they've only just met he feels proud of how much she is admired.

At one o'clock a number of the musicians pack away their instruments and Saoirse stands up to do the same. Tom takes her hand.

'Come on now, won't you stay a bit longer. Give us another song.'

She smiles. 'I've got to go. I'm not like you fellas up here anymore. Can't manage the late nights and I have to be up in the morning for the drive home.'

'So you won't be here next week then?'

'No I won't. I'm back at work on Monday. I'll be up again in the next holidays.'

'That's far too long. I'm down at Croke Park for the game in a couple of weeks. Would you be around?'

Saoirse laughs and writes down her number. 'I might be, now give me a hand with this harp, will you?'

As they push their way through the side door of the bar and out to her car, Tom tilts his head to one side. 'Before you go might I ask you a question?'

'Fire away.'

'Can I ask you how you like your carrots?'

Ruby Red Soldiers
Darren Gallagher

Clara opened the door and stepped out into the warm sunshine. The soft breeze brushed her skin and threw the scent of summer toward her. A perfect morning to stretch her old bones and get to know her neighbours.

She walked down the garden path as a postman pulled up in his van.

'Missus Prange?' he asked.

'I am.' Clara smiled.

'I've a parcel for you.' He held a box out the window.

'You wouldn't be a dear and leave that just inside the door would you? These old legs of mine don't work as well as they used to.'

The postman got out, clearly unimpressed, and left the parcel in the hallway.

'Thank you,' Clara said as he passed by.

He got into his van and drove off without responding.

Clara couldn't help but think he was rude. She

decided then and there she'd let him suffer; spoilt children need to be taught a lesson after all.

With that sorted, she wondered which direction she should go. Houses lined the street on both sides. She spied a woman gardening directly across the road. Clara crossed over and walked right up to the picket fence.

'Good morning,' she said, startling the little woman, who was pushing bulbs into the earth.

'Oh, good morning,' the woman said, placing one hand on her chest to ease the fright back in.

"Sorry, I didn't mean to frighten you,' Clara said.

'No, no, it's okay. I was daydreaming and forgot about reality there for a moment.' The woman laughed, but she let out a heavy sigh as she stood up.

'Everything okay?'

'I'm fine. This old knee of mine plays up every now and again when I kneel on it for too long.' She took off her gardening gloves and reached her hand out to Clara. 'Hi, I'm Anna.'

'Nice to meet you, Anna. I'm Clara. You know, I have something that would clear your knee right up.'

'Really? I've tried everything - nothing works.'

'Well, come on over this evening, and we'll see if my remedy works for you.' Clara's smile didn't quite reach her eyes. 'And if not, we can have a cuppa and a little chat.'

'I'd love that.' Anna smiled back.

'Great,' Clara said. 'I'm sorry to be rude, but I must be heading on. I have to get a few things from town. It was lovely to meet you.'

'Nice to meet you, too,' Anna said. 'I'll see you this evening.'

'I look forward to it.'

Clara went on down the street. She was happy; the encounter had been easier than expected. People these days were far too trusting, not like the old days when you had to be careful. She laughed; this was *far* too easy. She set off to find more victims.

***

Clara walked aimlessly through the aisles of the local shop. She had already put a box of teabags, sugar, and a packet of biscuits into her shopping basket. She had no desire for such things, but at times it was useful to have these essentials around. Grabbing a litre of milk from the fridge, she made her way toward the till.

'Good afternoon,' a man said, as she placed the basket on the counter.

'Afternoon.' She tried her smile on him.

'I don't believe I've seen you in here before. Just passing through?'

'No, I've bought a little cottage just up the road there. You'll be seeing a lot more of me, I'm afraid.'

'Delighted to hear it. My name's Malcolm.' He offered his hand.

'Clara.' She noticed that he had a firm grip, one she wasn't used to.

'So, what made you move to our little corner of

the world?' Malcolm asked, as he scanned the items and placed them into a bag.

'It seemed like a nice, quiet little town, somewhere I could relax.'

'You've come to the right place.' Malcolm said. He was pleasant, Clara thought.

Clara paid him and lifted the bags. 'It was nice to meet you, Malcolm, see you around.'

She was smiling again as she left the shop. She had another potential victim, although she didn't know how to catch him yet.

She walked home with the groceries in the warm sunshine. Luckily it wasn't too far and the milk didn't sour. The front door to her house was still open. No one had entered since the postman. His scent still lingered, untainted.

She put the groceries away. She had all the items a household would need, Daryl had seen to that. It was important to remain inconspicuous, he said. Clara didn't care; soon no one would be asking questions.

She took the parcel into the kitchen and opened it with a knife. Inside were dozens of little glass vials, racks to hold them, a glass dropper and a glass beaker. Clara half-filled the beaker with water from the sink, held her left hand over it and lifted the knife. Closing her fist tightly around the blade, she pulled it out violently.

She didn't even flinch as her blood ran into the beaker. Diluting in the water, the blood filtered its way to the bottom, and Clara continued to let it drip until most of the water had turned red. Finally, she began licking the blood from the open wound then watched as it closed up, leaving no evidence that it was ever there.

She stirred the contents of the beaker with the knife until the mixture of blood and water turned a ruby red.

She put the knife down on the table and lifted a vial and unscrewed the cap. Using the dropper, she carefully removed some of the ruby liquid from the beaker and transferred it into the vial. After sealing the vial with a small cap, Clara held it up in front of her face and smiled. She had a feeling this town would be interesting, and it would all start tonight with Anna.

Clara repeated the process until the beaker was emptied into the vials. Dozens of little ruby red soldiers were laid out on the table, waiting to be called upon.

Delighted everything was ready, she got up and cleared the table. She couldn't have this lying around if she was going to have visitors. Clara finished by lining up her little soldiers at the edge of the cupboard above the cooker. She closed the press door and went into the sitting room where she relaxed, satisfied, in her armchair as the day rolled on toward evening.

***

'Hello.' A friendly voice called into the house, accompanied by a rap on the door.

Clara got up and walked into the hallway. Anna was standing just outside her door. She wouldn't cross the threshold, though Clara had left the door wide open.

'Come in, come in.' She beckoned Anna.

'Thank you.' Anna stepped in. 'This is for you.' She handed Clara a cooking dish with a tea cloth over it. 'I thought we might have a little treat with our tea.'

'It smells wonderful.' Clara could already taste the sweet apples that lay beneath.

Anna followed her through to the kitchen. They had tea and some pie. It was as tasty as it smelled, but Clara had no desire for it. Eating was nothing more than keeping up appearances.

After their tea, Clara walked over to the press and lifted down one of the little red vials. Returning to the table she handed it to Anna.

'Take this when you go home, and that bothersome knee of yours will no longer give you trouble.'

'What is it?' Anna looked at it, confused.

'It's just a little something I made up. It has helped many people in the past, and I'm sure it will do the same for you.'

'Thank you. You sure it will work?'

'Positive.'

Anna was delighted; she hated it when her knee seized up. She was willing to try anything that would help.

She stayed and chatted for a little while,

revealing that the postman was Charles, her husband. Apparently, Charles was rude all the time because of his lower back pain. Once she had gone, Clara went into the sitting room. She didn't bother turning on the light. What was about to happen had greater effects when it was dark.

Getting comfortable in her armchair, she closed her eyes and waited. It wouldn't be long.

Five minutes later, images and thoughts flooded into her head. Everything Anna had ever experienced, Clara could see it too. All of Anna's most intimate thoughts were revealed to her and she revelled in it. Step one was complete. Anna's knee would no longer give her trouble, for Clara's blood in small doses had great healing properties.

Anna would pass on the word about her wonderful tonic to everyone, including Charles, but Clara would let him suffer that little bit longer.

***

The next morning, as Clara went for another stroll through town, Anna ran across the street and thanked her. She had no idea how Clara had done it, but she felt like she was young again. Clara smiled; she knew Anna's deepest, dirtiest secrets. That was the only thanks she needed.

Walking through town she noticed a park, and thought she would stop for a rest. The park was pretty big, and in the centre there was a large pond with ducks, and a spray of water shooting from the centre. It was pretty, and Clara sat on one of the benches to admire it.

A few minutes later she noticed a woman walking, or rather stumbling her way. She sat down heavily beside Clara and let out an exasperated sigh.

'You okay, dear?' Clara asked.

'Not really, but I'll come around in a minute.' The woman was breathing heavily.

'What's wrong with you? If you don't mind me asking.'

The woman looked at her, but her eyes had trouble focusing. 'I have dizzy spells every now and again. It'll pass.'

'I have something that will help you, if you want it?' Clara pulled one of her ruby soldiers out of her pocket.

'What is it?'

'It's just a little tonic.'

'Sorry, I don't know you, and that could be anything,' the woman said, as she began to come around.

'That's okay, but if you change your mind just let me know.' Clara smiled at her.

'Sure.'

They sat staring at the pond and the ducks while the woman recuperated.

'Beautiful day, isn't it?' Clara said, breaking the silence.

'It's just a pity I can't enjoy it more.'

'Your dizzy spells that bad?'

'Unfortunately.'

'That must be a nightmare. I'm Clara, by the way.'

'Maria.' They shook hands. 'Sorry, I must be on my way again. It was nice meeting you.'

Maria stood up slowly, and once she was sure she wasn't going to get dizzy, she smiled at Clara and walked away. Clara was disappointed. She had failed to get another victim, but she knew when the word got around, she'd see Maria again.

***

Clara bumped into Malcolm on her way home, as he unloaded stock from his car. He stopped and politely stuck up a conversation with her. She was happy about that; she liked getting to know a person before devouring their secrets. It made them that little bit more desirable.

Once she got home, she settled into her armchair.

Sometime later, she heard her front door open softly, and the sound of quiet footsteps entering the house.

'Boo!' came a voice from behind her.

'Daryl, how many times do I have to tell you? That doesn't work on me.'

'Ah, you're no fun.' He walked around and seated himself on the sofa across from her. 'So ... how's it going?'

'Good. I've got one, the rest will soon follow.'

'That was fast. Have you eaten?'

'Not yet.'

'You know you can't go long without.'

'I've been around a lot longer than you. I know how to take care of myself.'

'Sure, but just in case. Give me a few vials and I'll pass them around to the local addicts.'

'They're in the kitchen.'

Daryl left the room, and soon Clara could hear him opening and closing cabinet doors. He'd find them - eventually.

'Okay, they'll think it's a drug, so when you receive, push a little back,' he said.

'Daryl, don't you remember who taught you all this?'

He laughed and knelt beside her. 'You did, but you're getting old, and even though you are an Original, there are side effects for staying alive so long. Especially if you don't feed.'

Clara raised her hand to his cheek. 'The others experimented too much with their own bodies; they wanted to be so much more than we already are. That's why there are side effects with Originals. You've no need to worry about me.' She smiled.

'I hope not. I'll be back in a few days, but in the meantime, have something to eat will you? Let's not take the risk.'

'Fine, go do what you have to do.'

Daryl left, and within fifteen minutes she was receiving the thoughts and secrets from four teenagers. As Daryl had suggested, she pushed back the feeling of euphoria so they would believe, then she took in every little detail of their lives. Clara couldn't believe some of the things these teenagers had done, but she laughed at it. She held their thoughts for a while and then called to one of the young men, telling him to come over. She knew he would obey. She controlled them now.

****

Over the next few days, word spread of the miracle cure. People approached her on the street and Clara happily gave them her little ruby red soldiers. She loved devouring their secrets; each one filled another little piece of the huge puzzle unravelling before her. And whenever she was hungry, she only had to call.

Charles approached her one day asking for help, all nice and sincere. Amused, Clara told him she was out of stock and it would be a few days before she had more.

The next night, Clara found Maria on the doorstep. She was barely able to hold herself up against the wall. Clara gently took her arm and seated her on the sofa.

'You okay, dear?'

'No.' Maria tried to shake her head. 'Help, please?'

Clara retrieved one of the vials and poured the

liquid into Maria's mouth.

Maria's eyes focused on Clara and her body became sturdy.

'I can't believe this is real.' She looked stunned. 'How'd you do that?'

'Don't you worry about that.' Clara smiled.

'When do the effects wear off?'

'They don't.'

'I don't believe you.'

'Just wait and see.'

Maria started to laugh and jumped up onto her feet. 'I haven't been able to do that since I was a little girl.' She twirled herself around. 'Thank you so much.'

'You're welcome dear. Now go and enjoy it.'

Maria was happy to oblige. Before leaving she turned and hugged Clara; then ran off into the night.

Clara had just sat down when another knock sounded. When she opened the door Charles was standing there.

'Hi,' he said nervously.

'Yes?' Clara hissed. She hated beggars and made no attempt to hide her annoyance.

'I was wondering if you had a new batch.'

'New batch of what?'

'Of that tonic stuff you gave my wife.' Charles looked desperate.

Clara didn't want to give in to him so soon, but she didn't want him constantly on her back either. She went and grabbed one of her little ruby soldiers.

'Take this when you get home, no sooner. Okay?'

Clara said intensely.

'I will. Thank you, thank you. Thank you so much,' Charles said, his words running into each other.

'Sure, now go home.'

Before Charles had his back turned, Clara had the door closed. She didn't get time to rejoice in the last one. She might as well savour this.

Clara now held the secrets of over half of the townspeople. They were under her control if she so desired. Still, there was one she had not captured. Malcolm, the shopkeeper, had never once approached her about her remedy. She needed to devise a plan to get him; he was the only one left that she actually desired.

Clara pushed those thoughts aside and focused at the time at hand. The vial she had given Charles was opened, now was the time to relax and take in his life.

***

'Good afternoon, Clara,' Malcolm greeted, as she walked into the shop.

'Hello, Malcolm. How are you?' she said, but there was no life in her voice.

'I'm good, and how could I not be with a day like that.'

'Is it always this good?' she asked, taking a basket.

'In the summer, yes. Not so nice in the winter, though.'

'I better get prepared then.' She laughed.

Proceeding down one of the aisles, Clara grabbed several heavy items and piled them into the basket. By the time she got to the counter she was struggling to hold it.

'Here, let me get that for you.' Malcolm reached for the groceries.

'Oh, thank you. I don't know what's wrong with me today, I just feel so weak.' Clara put the back of her hand to her forehead.

'If you don't mind my asking, how are you getting home?'

'Walking, of course.'

'I'll give you a lift, can't have you carrying these all the way home.'

'Oh no, you don't have to do that. I'll be fine.'

'I insist.'

Malcolm called to someone in the backroom. A teenage girl came out and took over the till. His daughter, Clara assumed - another secret waiting to be unveiled.

***

Malcolm parked just outside her house and carried in her groceries.

'Will you stay for a cup of tea? It's the least I can do to thank you,' she said, as he placed the bags on the table.

'I really should get back to the shop.'

'But it's only one wee cup - it won't take that

long.'

'Go on then.' Malcolm smiled and took a seat at the table.

'Excellent.' She flicked the switch on the kettle and it started to boil, then she grabbed two cups from the press beside the little ruby soldiers.

'Do you take sugar?' she asked, dropping a teabag in each cup.

'No thanks.'

Malcolm was looking around the room. It was the perfect opportunity to pour the ruby liquid into his cup.

'That was awful nice of you to bring me home. Do you do that with all your customers?'

'Just the ones in need.'

The kettle clicked off.

Clara poured the water, put the kettle back on its hub, and concealed the empty vial behind it.

She handed Malcolm the cup and sat down at the table.

'Thank you.' He lifted the cup to his lips.

Clara waited in anticipation - her plan was just about to be completed. Any second now his deepest desires would be revealed. She was so excited, she couldn't help but grin.

Malcolm took a sip.

She braced herself for the rush of images. Nothing came.

He took another drink.

Clara expected them to come this time, but again,

nothing. Maybe none of it had gotten through. Maybe there had been too much dilution.

'Are you okay?' he asked, 'You look a little pale.'

'Yeah, I'm fine,' she replied, in a low caught up voice. 'Just one of those days, you know.'

'I do indeed.' Malcolm took another gulp of tea.

Clara looked across at him, baffled.

How can this be happening? Why is this happening?

He placed the cup on the table. 'Tell me, how can you walk in the sun?'

She was confused by his question. 'The same way as everyone else, I suppose.'

'But vampires can't walk in the sun.' He was looking her dead in the eye.

Clara was stunned. She tried to conceal it.

How the hell did he know?

'I'm sorry; I don't know anything about vampires.'

'Now, now, don't try to play games. I mean, wouldn't you like to know why your precious *tonic* has no effect on me? Oh, and before you say you don't know what I'm talking about, there's an empty vial behind the kettle. Your blood was in that vial before you put it in my cup.'

Clara could only look at him. She had no idea how he knew that.

'So, how do you walk in the sun?'

'I'm an Original,' Clara said, feeling confident again.

'An Original.'

'We're the first of our kind, the ones who existed before tainted experiments turned the others into what they are now.'

'Ah,' Malcolm said.

'And what are you?'

'Haven't you figured it out yet?' Malcolm teased.

'You're a wolf aren't you? A werewolf?'

'Unlike your pitiful species, the evolution of werewolves has made us stronger, faster, and smarter, than our ancestors. I am a Lycan.' There was pride in Malcolm's voice.

He stood up. 'And I've had enough of you poisoning my home.'

Clara laughed. 'You don't scare me. You can't do anything to me in your human form.'

'You didn't hear me. I'm not a werewolf.'

Malcolm's bones started snapping and a snout began to push outwards from his jaw. Lines of spiked teeth forced their way down from his gums as thick, spiky hair shot out all over his body.

Clara stood, horrified. She retreated, only to find herself up against the wall.

Within seconds Malcolm had fully transformed. He advanced toward her, teeth bare and snarling, huge claws ready to rip flesh apart. A deep growl vibrated up out of his chest.

As he pounced on Clara, all across town injuries, illness and disease returned.

Friends

Sally Neary

The roof lifted off Mac's bar when Ireland beat Bosnia and Herzegovina to qualify for the European football championships. The draw to determine who plays who and where would be made in December 2015. Patsy knew this was it. He hummed the old Elvis Presley song, '*It's now or never....*' as he left Mac's. He had passed the evening, as usual, in the company of his two lifelong friends, Willie and Doncy. They considered themselves the best supporters and fans of the Irish soccer team, although they had never attended a match. They each had their own chair in front of the television, an uninterrupted viewing position. They liked to arrive a good hour before kickoff. It was important to have at least two pints enjoyed before the action started. The highlights of their lives, the three agreed.

Patsy had made them a promise: If Ireland ever qualified he would see to it that the three would travel to at least one of the matches. The trouble was that the matches were being played in France. Patsy calculated the cost: There was the bus to Dublin, €20; flights to France, well over €100; match tickets, God only knows; not to mention drinking money to see them safely home again.

'Money,' he said aloud to no one other than the ticking kitchen clock. 'It'll all cost money.'

Patsy wanted to raise the subject with Willie and Doncy when they were next on the Back to Work scheme. He thought it was a strange name for the re-employment programme as none of them had ever worked a day in their lives, well not that anyone in the dole office knew about. Their friendship went back to the first year they started school.

They looked nothing alike. Patsy, shy with his uncut mop of blond curls, had already spent six months at school, which gave him an assumed air of seniority. Then there was Willie, a patch over one eye held in place by wire-rimmed glasses that sat beneath bowl-cut ginger hair; and Patrick Joseph, as he was then known, who had prominent upper teeth and hands that were so filled with warts that none of the girls wanted to sit too close. That suited the three boys, who preferred the seats at the back of the classroom. They acknowledged each other's lack of social ease and smelled the familiar smell of poverty, instinctively recognising a kindred spirit. Schoolwork did not come easy to any of the three. Yet they knew how to milk and fodder cattle, could tell you where the fattest salmon were to be found and could pull an oar almost as well as any man.

Patrick Joseph loved history, especially the talk of battles and blood. One day as school plodded into the final hour before home time at three o'clock, the slaying of Ireland's High King, Brian Boru, absorbed his attention. The class stilled in fear of one of the Master's rages, their breaths captive in their thin, young bodies. Any child who looked the wrong way, coughed, moved or offered the wrong answer to the Master's questions risked being called up in front of the class. They were ordered to hold their outstretched hand to receive their due 'payment', a stroke of his cane brought down with his full force. A child who winced or withdrew their hand to avoid the slap earned double punishment.

'So how did the Viking manage to creep into Brian Boru's tent as he knelt to pray, killing him with one stroke?' the Master's voice boomed out.

From the back of the class came an unfamiliar voice. Patrick Joseph, wedged three-to-a-seat between Willie and Patsy, shouted, 'Doncy.

'It was very doncy,' he said, referring to the good fortune and chance which favoured the Viking.

Silence. The class waited for the usual eruption. Instead the Master broke into manic laughter.

'Doncy,' he shouted. 'Patrick Joseph Boyle. It is you who are doncy.'

And so Patrick Joseph lost the name chosen by his parents and acquired the one which carried him through life.

***

The boys lived in each other's shadows. They accepted the lack of luxury in their lives and never complained when the basics were also absent. Their diet consisted of porridge for breakfast, boiled potatoes for dinner, bread and jam for tea. Friday dinner may have offered salty fish to go with the potatoes. Roast chicken on Sundays was a big treat. Their clothes were hand-me-downs and had lost any semblance of fashion or heat value. Scarce toys were treasured. So if a comic, toy soldier or Corgi car was borrowed it was returned in the condition it was given in.

The only thing the boys ever envied was the fact that Willie had a father. Willie frequently started a sentence with, 'When my Da comes home …'

Between themselves, Patsy and Doncy agreed that maybe Willie had imagined him. Then, one summer evening, off the bus stepped a tall, thin man who had Willie's pale face, freckles and red hair. There the resemblance seemed to end for this was an exotic creature. He sported a shiny suit of pale grey with matching narrow tie and brilliant white shirt. None of the local men wore a suit and if they did it was as near to black as was possible. Although raised in the next parish, this visitor had lost any Irish inflection in his speech. In the days following his arrival, Patsy and Doncy discussed the new sensation in the area, Willie's dad. They thought he sounded peculiar but would not say this to their good friend Willie.

'All right, mate,' was his greeting. He used strange words and talked about a "guv" as in 'we was in this pub, right, and the guv frew us out.'

The boys were charmed by him and loved to be in his company. They basked in Willie's reflected glory and watched as Willie's dad, as he liked to be called, joked with Willie, tousling his hair. Willie beamed from ear to ear, adoring, happy to be in his father's slipstream. Yes, a father was a great thing to have. The boys could not believe their luck when Willie's dad invited them to the Ritz cinema, Killybegs. "The Magnificent Seven" was showing.

They had often played cowboys but nothing prepared them for Living Technicolour, the fast horses and the good guys shooting dead the bad and saving the entire town. For weeks afterwards the boys played many games of cowboy, each one fancying themselves as Yul Brynner or Steve McQueen and only grudgingly taking turns being the bad guy. Many years later Patsy would recall the sight of those men dying right in front of his eyes and vowed whatever way they would get money, no one would die in the process.

But that evening no expense was spared. Willie's father bought sweets and ice cream in quantities the boys had never imagined. Then when they were fit to burst they went to Melly's chip shop and each had a portion of large chip and battered sausage. They were never happier.

Patsy woke the next morning still full and humming the great tune from the film. He rushed over to Willie's. But he was struck rigid by the sound of a woman crying before he reached the front door. It was Willie's ma. Willie stood his mouth open like a fish that had just been caught.

'He's gone. He's away back to London,' Willie said after a long time.

'Sure he'll be back. He said so. Said he couldn't wait to get home again at Christmas.'

Patsy comforted his friend. In their hearts they knew the truth of it. Christmas came and went but no sign of dad and worse still, no letter with money in it. Willie's ma wrote to the only address she had for her husband, letting him know that Willie would become a big brother, but the postman never stopped at Sweeney's with a letter bearing the Queen's head.

Mary Josephine arrived looking very like Willie. But the resemblance was in looks only, for this baby sister was fiery and feisty. When she could walk she trailed after the three boys who initially resented her presence. They learned to accept that Willie had to look after her when his mother went to work. They taught her all they knew about the important things: Who was the fastest gun in the west, how to load caps into a gun, how to pick up a crab and not get nipped. They passed on their collective knowledge about fighting but she far excelled any of the boys in her viciousness and earned a reputation as a fearless opponent even when her adversary was twice her size.

'Hit him, Mary Joe, hit him,' frequently reverberated on their walk home from school, as a mismatched pair squared off. It would be Mary Joe, small and wiry, against the biggest boy who would take her on. But she still hadn't been born when Willie had his finest hour. One bitter March day, the schoolyard was full. Willie found himself on the wrong side of the school bully, John Joe Doherty. Although no one stopped their play all eyes were on the pair. Willie was in a corner and Patsy could hear him say, 'My da'll be home next month, John Joe Doherty, and he'll sort you out.'

Doherty's sneer showed he was having none of it.

'Your da! Your da, that's all you're good for, Sweeney. My uncle Danny says that your precious da is in a big prison called Wormwood Scrubs and anyway when he gets out, if he ever does, he'll go back to his other woman, a wog. Do you think he'll come back to you and your smelly mother?'

Patsy was about to ask, 'What's a wog?', when he caught sight of Willie's fist making violent contact with John Joe's face. He gasped at the sight of Doherty flat out on the ground, blood pouring from his mouth. But it was Willie's face that said it all, crumpled in grief, the loss of his special dad and all the hope he invested in him gone in one instant. Patsy and Doncy followed Willie home. The boys walked solemnly, as in a funeral procession, heads bowed. No one spoke. Willie never mentioned his dad again.

***

The thing Patsy missed most was not having a father. One day while eating his potatoes after school he broached a subject that had been on his mind for some time.

'Ma. What's a bastard?'

His mother answered without lifting her head from the washtub, her hands red from the carbolic soap she used for the washing she took in as her only source of income.

'Them what calls you it. Remember that, Patsy. Them what calls you it are no good. Us O'Donnells are dacent people, hardworking and honest. You, Patsy, are the best son any mother could have. Always remember that and hold your head high.'

His mother's words stayed with Patsy. He carried them into adulthood.

***

Fish and chips was their treat on Fridays when Patsy had collected his mum's pension. Now a grown man, he watched his mother, grey head bowed.

'Them's right good chips the day, Patsy,' she said as she licked a salty one.

He wanted to tell her that she was the best mother anyone could ever have, that he now knew the sacrifice she had made to keep and rear him herself in a time and community that judged and belittled mothers who were unmarried. But all he managed to say was, 'You're right Ma. They're right good the day, right good.'

Patsy was close to his mother. In her frail old age he was her only carer. They liked to sit and talk. She loved it when he brought her all the news. If she was still awake when he came home from the pub he'd make her a cup of tea so he could watch her dunk her favourite biscuits. But he never shared his deepest wish to see Ireland play. He couldn't tell her that he could think of nothing else, now that Ireland had qualified. How would he manage to get himself and his best friends, the two closest to him after his mother, away to matches like so many of the Irish fans he had seen on television?

***

Patsy, Willie and Doncy had never travelled abroad. All three had been to Dublin twice to see Donegal play in Croke Park. It took them three days to get home and they lost Willie in Cavan. That was a minor matter. Patsy had known Willie would return in one piece. Sure enough, a week later he stepped off the bus looking dishevelled, grinning from ear to ear and thanking the bus driver for the lift. Patsy didn't want to know but Doncy had a story about Willie meeting the love of his life outside a pub in Virginia and following her to Ballyjamesduff. All seemed to be going well till her husband returned and ruined the lovers' tryst. No, Patsy would have to manage the boys and take care of them when they were away from home. But first, passports were needed.

Patsy knew this would not be a problem. It being an election year, he only had to ask the first electoral candidate to canvass and the three passports were as good as got. No, money was the real problem. He knew Doncy was the only one to have a bank account. His mother, the late Mrs. Boyle, had opted to open a joint account with Doncy into which her pension was paid. He had overheard a conversation in the pub about how good the Credit Union was at lending out money, so he thought his problem was solved until he realised that the prospective borrower had to have a history of saving. Quick money was not easy come by. He read about Tiger kidnappings. He had thought seriously about the three of them kidnapping the old major. Sure wasn't he nearly dead already? He must be worth a bob or two into the bargain. Somehow Patsy could not take himself to plan on harming any creature, never mind another human being. The time to buy their match tickets, plan and pay for their journey was drawing near. He gave up any hope of managing to raise the money. Willie and Doncy picked up on his mood. Their only regret was that they could not provide any financial help.

***

One wet Saturday morning in late May, trees were struggling against an unseasonable Atlantic gale that stripped the protective sheaths off new leaves. Patsy was still in bed when he heard a familiar tap on the back kitchen window.

Doncy and Willie were standing at the back door. Patsy sensed something was amiss.

'What has ye out on a wild morning like this?' Both ignored his question.

'Show him Doncy, show him.'

Reluctantly Doncy produced an envelope from his jacket pocket. With deep gravity he opened it to reveal a cheque. He handed it to Patsy, who read that it was made out for the sum of three thousand euro, made payable to Mr Patrick Joseph Boyle. The three knew that this was a local, well-to-do businessman.

'I … I … I fo-fo-found it just ly-lying on the ro-road. S-s-see that is my p-p-proper name. All my official d-d-documents have that name on it. It-it's a sign, Patsy. Th-this was meant for us.' Doncy's speech impediment emerged when excited.

'A-a-all is we have to do is to take this to the bank. They'll give me the m-money, I know. We'll take it to the bank in Donegal town where me and ma have a savings account. They know me as P-P-Patrick Joseph. The girls in the bank call me that when they are out on their lu-lu-lunch-break.'

Patsy wasn't sure. This was forgery, which could land them in court, maybe worse still, prison. He had not considered Willie's position.

'Jeschrist man what have we to lose? That wanker Boyle, driving around in his big Mercedes; the wife with her Hyundai Coupé and his fancy woman, whose arse is only the size of a shirt button, driving around in a big Pajero. All of them so stuck up they wouldn't give ye the steam off their piss. Three thousand is only chicken feed to him; he'll never miss it.'

Patsy and Doncy nodded their heads in solemn agreement as though Willie had just quoted a verse of sacred scripture. Patrick Joseph Boyle was known to be ruthless, a man who had a keen nose for a good deal and no moral compass. Many marvelled at his ability to keep his wife and 'fancy woman' in a permanent dance of avoidance as he grinned his way through slippery business ventures that left more than one of his creditors at a loss.

Patsy could feel a rush of blood; he felt his heart had overruled his head. This was their one chance and he couldn't allow it to pass. 'By Christ we'll do it. We'll fuckin' do it. Are yez in?'

The question was redundant. The animated expressions on the other two faces said it all.

'We'll all head to the bank this Monday, not leave Doncy here to do the dirty work. It might take a few days for the cheque to go through. We'll just sit tight till it does. In the meantime we'll have to think about tactics,' Patsy said.

A great deal of talk followed about getting buses, booking flights, procuring match tickets. No firm plan emerged until the Sunday midday pint in Mac's.

'I heard about boys travelling to matches in Hiace vans,' Patsy offered. 'Now think about it. It's not as silly as it sounds. A good mattress in the back and we have our transport and a place to sleep sorted.'

'Willie here is not a bad driver. Remember them French drive on the wrong side of the road. You could manage that? Sure, what am I talking about; didn't you drive a truck for McLean's for a few years? Piece of cake to you, Willie boy. Piece of cake.'

Willie beamed. Where to get the van? That was the next problem.

Willie was in deep conversation with a young fella from Laghey. 'I'm telling ye, Westwood wouldn't be half the man Given can be. He was on fire when he played for City.'

There was something slightly strange about this football pundit Patsy wasn't sure about. His head was shaved from his ear to his temples, leaving a mop of fine healthy hair falling down to one side. It wasn't the tattoos that decorated his arms that alarmed Patsy; no, it was the smell. That was not natural for a man to smell so perfumed like a woman. But this fella was talking about a van for sale in Ballintra, one owner, clean, a sweet machine in any man's language.

***

All night Patsy worried. How would it go when they got to the bank? Would their deception be discovered? A young teller Willie did not recognise cashed the cheque, no awkward questions asked. They all agreed it was probably her first week in the bank. Then they had to wait. By ten thirty on Monday of the following week they were in a taxi heading to buy the van in Ballintra. Driving home the excitement built up like a giant balloon: Willie at the wheel; Doncy, arms folded across his chest trying to contain his joy; Patsy, urging Willie to drive slowly.

'Go easy for Christ's sakes. We haven't tax or insurance or buck all on this thing. If we're stopped by the guards we're sunk.'

They were headed home but Patsy took little persuading to 'stop in Dom's just for one.' The one lasted till the small hours and the last thing he remembered was singing, 'Come on you boys in green, come on you boys in green,' with his arms around some American lady who 'just loved Ireland'.

***

His head was thumping the next morning. At first he didn't hear the loud banging on the front door, but the sound sobered and frightened him. He opened the door to McAuley, the local Garda sergeant. Patsy had shared a pint with McAuley in the past and thought of him as a right sort of a guard who wouldn't do you any harm. Now Patsy wasn't sure.

Patsy showed him into the sitting room.

'Mammy likes to sleep in the mornings. Sometimes her pains are bad at night,' he said by way of explanation.

'We'll not disturb her now, Patsy,' Sergeant

McCauley said kindly. 'I have a small matter to discuss with you. Yesterday morning at approximately 10:05, Patrick Joseph Boyle, known as Doncy, and Willie Sweeney presented a cheque at Ulster Bank, Donegal town, for €3,000. They were accompanied by a third man. I believe that man to be you.'

In the silence that followed Patsy tried to utter a word, any word, but his mouth felt like cotton wool and his brain not much better. McAuley continued.

'I have reason to believe you then went on to purchase a navy or dark-coloured Hiace van, registration number 01 DL 2963, the same van which is now parked outside Mr Sweeney's house and which, by the way has no tax, insurance or NCT disk.'

Still no sound from Patsy. All his concentration seemed to wilt.

'Now Patsy, I needn't tell you this is a serious matter. For a start I know that the cheque was made out to Patrick Joseph Boyle, businessman, not your friend Doncy. I was alerted by the bank and checked with Mr Boyle's office who confirmed that a cheque for this amount had been mislaid by one of the girls from his office. This is impersonation, forgery and theft. A crime has been committed. I wouldn't like to see you three boys going before the judge. You could get time and I don't think any of the three of you would be fit for it.'

'I have already spoken with your two friends, Patsy. They have come clean. So no use denying any of it. I'll be back. No need to get up. I know where the door is.'

Patsy couldn't move. But then he had to rush head first to the kitchen sink, where the contents of his stomach landed on top of yesterday's saucepans.

'You alright, son?' Ma's voice sounded weaker.

'I'm grand, Ma,' he lied. 'I'll get you your tea in a wee minute.'

The kettle was hardly boiled when the first familiar rap, and then the second, came to the back kitchen window. Willie and Doncy stood before him, both pale and shaking. Doncy seemed to have the edge in pallor.

'Christ Patsy, we're fucked,' Willie seemed to express for all three.

"B-b-bollixed," Doncy echoed his sentiments.

'The thing is …,' Willie started but couldn't seem to finish his sentence.

Mechanically Patsy made four cups of strong, sweet tea and a plateful of toast. The boys ate in silence and left. Patsy attended to his elderly mother with his usual care and kindness. Not one word of his dilemma did he whisper to her.

The following days were bleak. Patsy did not relish the idea of going to jail but his greatest regret was that he had let his friends down. Wasn't he always the sensible one? The one who looked out for the other two. He should have refused to go along with that stupid cheque business, been wiser on behalf of those who mattered most. They were not the kind of people who travelled away for anything. What was he thinking about sure, none of them had ever left Ireland and they probably never would now, not with a criminal record.

***

One evening the following week, the three were nursing half pints in Mac's when Willie's phone rang.

Mary Joe normally did not call on a weekday. But she had received an email from John Joe Doherty's son, Cathal, alerting her to the boys' dilemma. On her rise to the top of New York's banking world she had lost most of her Irish inflections. Now, as the door to her director's office slid closed behind her, she reverted to her native tongue.

'For fuck's sakes, Willie. What were you thinking? Mammy is turning in her grave. The Sweeneys never had nothing but we were honest. John Joe says you could all go to prison. What did you need the money for so badly?'

Willie heard his voice say feebly, 'Football.'

'Football,' Mary Joe roared incredulously. 'Are Donegal in the Ulster final again?'

Patsy gestured to Willie to hand him the phone. 'Mary Joe. It is good to talk to you …'

'Patsy, I thought you would have more sense than allow those two buck eejits to hatch a plan like this.' Mary Joe had found the raw nerve.

'You see, Ireland qualified for the European championships and me and the boys thought we'd like to go.' Patsy knew he sounded sheepish.

'You? Where?' Mary Joe asked, more reasonable now.

'Well the first game is in Paris but me and the boys will probably not manage to get tickets but the next one in Lille ...'

'Paris, Lille! Jeschrist you don't do things by half. So the only way you thought to do it was steal from that prick Boyle?'

'We'll pay him back. It was only ever meant to be a kind of loan,' Patsy lied.

It was the most unsatisfactory conversation the boys had had with Mary Joe. They felt chastened. Secretly they were proud she was still the same Mary Joe; just like John Wayne, she took no shit from no Indians.

***

Several black mornings later, Patsy woke to voices in the kitchen. *Christ I am being arrested*, he thought.

'Jesus,' he shouted, pulling on his trousers. But he found Willie and Doncy fully dressed, standing in the back kitchen with Cathal Doherty.

'Wait till ye hear this. Wait till ye hear this ...' Willie couldn't complete the sentence.

Cathal intervened. 'Mary Joe has sent the three of you plane tickets for Paris and tickets for the match and spending money. She emailed me all the details.'

Patsy had to sit down. He felt his knees were

going to give way.

'She even paid back the money to Boyle, said it was just all one big mistake. He's happy and all charges will be dropped.' Doncy looked relieved.

And so it was that the three boys caught the 5 a.m. bus to Dublin, flew to Beauvais airport and took a bus to Paris and on to Lille. They were seated in the Stade Pierre-Mauroy well ahead of kickoff. The boys had never seen so many people, so many Irish supporters. The chanting, 'Fields of Athenry' and 'Come on you boys in green,' and many more that cannot be repeated.

They were nearly hoarse before the match started.

They were on their seats and off their seats, but when Brady scored the winning goal for Ireland Patsy felt his heart would stop. Instead he just hugged Doncy and Willie, tears streaming down his face.

'Christ boys did yez ever think we'd see this day. Did yez ever bloody think?'

***

Naturally, Mac's threw a party to welcome them home. As they entered the pub Seamus, the most regular of the regulars, left his pint and met them at the door.

'We seen yez on the telly.'

This was the piéce de résistance for the boys after travelling so far to see Ireland play, to appear on the television. This was an event they could recall, one which would ensure they could be treated to a free pint for the rest of their lives.

'Aye we did see yez,' another customer remarked.

They were hard to miss: Willie in his green onesie covered in shamrock; Doncy, with the biggest green hat and fake orange beard; Patsy's luminous green jacket barely fitting over his over-large tummy; and the one tricolour wrapped round them.

Seamus was insistent. 'We seen yez boys, we fuckin' did.'

The Pocket Watch
Ann Garratt

I threw my borrowed suitcase into the boot and climbed in the black Daimler beside Joe Sweeney, our neighbour. He cherished his car like a baby, and inside it smelled strongly of leather and beeswax . My family were huddled together against the cold north wind that whistled around the gable of the house. They waved and shouted their goodbyes through the car window, but I could only focus on Mammy. Her eyes were fixed on me and she was staring, pleading. *Don't go.* Joe tapped my hand then slid into gear as the gravel crunched under the tyres when we pulled away. Our whitewashed thatched cottage, with its sweet, pink-tipped roses over the door, disappeared from view. I sighed and sank back on my seat, determined not to cry.

***

At my great age, time slips through my hands like sand, and the sky has grown dark and another day has passed. Each morning I sit here watching the seasons unfold before my weary eyes. It's spring now and the cherry tree is garlanded with pink. Beneath it the tulips, bobbing in the breeze, are every colour under the sun. Most days I spend here at the window. That's all I'm fit for, and more and more that image of Mammy from all those years ago, her fingers twisted around the hem of her black apron, keeps returning.

***

I just wanted to be left with my own thoughts that day, but you could hardly shut Joe up as we drove away from Donegal towards Belfast for the boat.

'A proud moment it must be for your mammy and your daddy. Often I prayed our Sarah had the calling but it was not to be,' Joe said, as he turned a broad smile to me. I nodded. I couldn't answer him, for my mind was too filled with the anguish and excitement of leaving. That morning, when I'd been washing the dishes, I'd argued with my mother.

'Sure I have a vocation.'

'Many's the one had a vocation but found the reality too much for them. The religious life can be harsh, it's not for everyone. They demand complete obedience. You've always been a rebel, determined to have the last word. They'll stifle you with their pater nosters and constant Hail Marys. Didn't your cousin Frances up and leave the convent after a few months.'

I turned, handing her a cup.

'Aye, and weren't her poor mother and father shamed. I'll not be doing the same to you.'

Mammy straightened herself, locking her eyes on mine.

'Don't be so sure of yourself. England's a different place altogether and so far away. Look at you, the baby of the family,' she said, her voice softening as she stroked my cheek.

'I'll get no peace if I think you're not content. So I've come up with a plan. The nuns are bound to censor your letters, so when you write home, just say, "Did you ever find Daddy's pocket watch?" Then I'll know you've had enough and want to leave.'

'But Daddy doesn't have a pocket watch.'

'I know,' she said, all pleased with herself. 'But if you write those words, we'll come and get you.'

I was silent for a moment, bitterly disappointed she didn't trust me to be sure of my own mind.

'I'll stick it,' I said, jutting out my chin.

'Promise me you'll remember – the pocket watch,' Mammy whispered, wagging her finger at me.

'There's no need. But if it keeps you happy I will.'

***

Even after all that happened, the decision to leave the convent wasn't easy. For months I prayed daily to Our Lady for guidance but found no answers. I shared my doubts in confession, but instead of the assistance I sought I was warned about the dangers to my immortal soul. I'd entered the order to care for the children in its charge, and I did my best. They were small, undernourished things, their eyes dull, spirits broken, and it pained me to see how they were treated by some of the other sisters. Believing the offspring of unmarried mothers to be tainted by sins of the flesh, most of the nuns despised their charges. So they bullied and beat them relentlessly.

There was one wee girl, Mary, a grey mousey dote of no more than eight or nine who I took a shine to. She was so frightened by the constant sniping that she was forever wetting the bed. One morning Sister Anthony, an old sister with small piggy eyes and a tight mouth, could hardly contain her rage. She grabbed the child by the hair and dragged her to the bathroom, shouting all the while, 'You dirty little tinker, I'd let you lie in it all day if it was up to me.'

Mary's bony shoulders heaved in fright. It was too much for me. I wrenched her away from the cruel nun and dried her tears. The child stared at me so sad and sorrowful, it broke my heart. Sister Anthony opened her mouth to speak but then closed it again, bubbling with rage. I lifted Mary into my arms and carried her to the bathroom. Running a warm bath, I placed the girl in it. She was trembling, but gave me a shy smile and I gently soaped her down. She never said a word but held onto me for life itself.

Later, I was called in to see the Reverend Mother. She listed the accusations Sister Anthony had made against me. It was then that the dam burst and I told her what I thought of her convent and her nuns. Her face turned purple and she ordered me out of her sight. Eventually it was decided I was only fit for scrubbing the floors and so I laboured from morning to night, hands raw, feeling exhausted and alone.

The letter home was harder than I thought. My emotions were as raw as my hands, and I felt a coward to be leaving the poor innocents. Tears stained the paper as I wrote to ask about the pocket watch, knowing in my heart that this was not the life for me. True to her word, Mammy came and I fell into her arms. There was quite a hullaballoo - the nuns did not give me up easily, they knew they'd failed in my vocation as much as I had. But my mother insisted.

At home I was the talk of the parish. My family tried their best to shield me from the worst of it, but wherever I went, our neighbours would fall silent and turn their heads away. Daddy was adamant, he told me to hold my head up, that I had nothing to be ashamed of, but I knew people would never let me forget. In the end Mammy gave me the fare.

'Ignore all this talk of a spoiled vocation. Go to England. Make a new life for yourself. Nobody there will know that you were a nun.'

***

I found a job as a maid in a hotel. It was after the war and I met Giles, my husband, there. He was one of the guests. Giles was handsome, with deep blue eyes and a low husky voice that made me quiver. He was well educated, an accountant by trade, and a Catholic like me. We had fifty years together until he died last year. Sadly it wasn't a happy union.

Soon after we after we married I discovered he had a temper and sometimes when we rowed he'd hit me. I kept it to myself but with every year that passed and every beating I endured, my heart grew harder. I never told him of my history, he wouldn't have understood. Stephanie, she's my eldest, only got it out of me a few months ago. All delighted, she was telling me that my grandson, Joseph, was going for the priesthood. I knew then I had to say something.

'But it doesn't always work out. It didn't for me.'

'Don't be ridiculous Mum, you weren't a priest,' she said, laughing.

'No, I wasn't.' I had to bite the bullet. 'But I was a nun for four years.'

My daughter narrowed her eyes.

'Run that past me again.' I told her the whole story.

'And did Daddy know?'

'No. In those days it was shocking, something you kept hidden. I was too ashamed to own up and as time went by it became harder.'

'But it's different now, so why didn't you tell me?'

I shook my head and sighed.

'I don't know. I should have.'

I reached out and took her hand, but she pulled it

away.

'I'm so disappointed you never told me before, Mum. But poor Daddy, he never knew. How could you have kept it a secret all those years?'

Tears sprung to my eyes. I begged Stephanie to try and appreciate my dilemma, but she only gathered her things together and left.

***

Stephanie and her father were very alike, both buttoned up. My grandson is a lovely boy, so kind and gentle, nothing like his grandfather. Joseph would understand. I love my daughter dearly, but we've never been close. She worshipped her father. I never told her he beat me and she probably wouldn't believe me if I had. Sometimes the truth isn't always easy to hear. The next time I saw Stephanie she apologised for her thoughtless words, saying she didn't blame me and she understood. And when I tried to explain further she tightened her mouth and told me she didn't want to talk about it.

A nice woman, Agatha, comes once a week and gives me Communion. She reads me the Sunday paper and I give her a few pounds - gifts for the children, I say. Last week she read me an article, and when I heard it I held my breath.

'They're looking for witnesses to the abuse that went on in the convents years ago. It's hard to believe some of the stories you hear. I mean, weren't the priests and nuns supposed to be caring for those youngsters?'

I smiled and nodded. I asked her for the paper as she was going, and she gladly handed it over.

'There's a wee bit I wanted to skip over again. I'll do it later when all the visitors have gone home.'

***

I read that article twenty times, trying to decide what to do. I've had no sleep for the last week, thinking about it. Outside my window the night is drawing in and the lounge is filled with the smell of cooked chicken. It's dinner time but I have no appetite, so I press the buzzer to call the Filipino nurse to take me to my room.

In a fitful sleep I dream of Mammy, but when I reach out to touch her I wake to find myself still in the chair by my bed. Reaching over to the cupboard beside me, I take out a package wrapped in tissue paper. A moment later I'm holding Daddy's silver pocket watch, a present I bought him with my wages that first Christmas after I came to England. Now I clasp it to my chest and think of them both and poor wee Mary.

Although I never really gave an explanation as to why I abandoned my vocation my parents didn't reproach me once. They were God-fearing people and they would want me to do the right thing. Stephanie will be angry with me for stirring it all up, and I'm sorry for that. But in my heart of hearts I know I have to speak out, to bear witness for Mary and all those poor children who never had a voice.

Into the Darkness
Malachy Sweeney

The place was buzzing, the music rocked the rafters and the dancers shook the floor in the little country hall. I checked my hair in the mirror, lashed on a good wallop of Brut and was ready to rock and roll. Between you and me, it was Mickey Gallagher who gave me the lowdown.

'It's a great wee spot, lively and ideal for a young fella like you. The girls are smashing, an' you never know who you'll meet.'

This was music to my ears. It was exactly what I wanted to hear. To be honest, the big hall in the town was too intimidating, with all the flashing lights and the mad stampede across the floor when a dance was called.

'I will admit,' he confided, 'it's not so good in wet weather, and almost impossible to chat up a girl when the rain batters off the tin roof. Lucky enough, the weather's settled at the minute and they're changing the thatch.'

Sure enough, Gallagher had it well sussed out and like he said, the hall was deadly, with a crowd that was friendly and game for a laugh. Mind you, the way I jived you had to have a good sense of humour. Near the last dance he sidled up to me and asked, 'Anything happening, chief?'

'No. Not really – but ...' I nodded towards a girl with long black hair and a tight red blouse. She was beautiful but I still hadn't plucked up enough courage. As usual, my old pal seemed to read my mind.

'It's the last dance,' he said, 'And you know what they say horse, nothing ventured, nothing gained.'

In my heart I cursed myself and wished I was more like him, with his swagger and carefree air.

'Take your partners for the last dance,' was the signal, and Gallagher was off like a hare. I thought, *sure, what the hell.* Then I pushed out my chest and shot after him.

I could see her across the floor and she looked better every step I took. Then a few people edged in front of me and I lost sight of her. It was the same old story - not determined enough, I knew, and I was gutted. There I stood, at the edge of the dance floor, trying to hide my disappointment and still hoping I looked casual and carefree. In the distance Gallagher glided around the floor and a girl leaned back in his arms and laughed. He was on a roll and I felt a twinge of envy and pride. He was my best friend.

With mixed feelings I turned away, but stopped in a wave of disbelief that I hoped didn't show. How could I have missed her? There she was, standing at my side. I even surprised myself when I held out my hand and heard myself saying, 'Would you care to dance?'

I'm still not sure what she said, but her face brightened into a shy smile. Our hands entwined and we stepped on to the floor. She slipped into my arms and our bodies melted together. When her firm breasts pushed against me, a surge of excitement coursed through my veins and all my doubts faded away. I knew immediately there was a heaven. She rested her head on my chest and I could feel her warm breath and the beat of her heart. Gallagher went gliding past, giving me a sly look and a nod of approval. I was on a roll; this night was different and one I would always remember. Little did I know.

We moved to the rhythm of the music, and not surprisingly, Canon Murphy's sermon ran through my head: Occasions of sin were a constant theme that he hammered home, week after week. If you even harboured an impure thought, it was a sin. *Anyway, what the hell.* We clung together, swayed with the music and floated around the floor.

The music stopped, she brushed back stray strands of hair, and whispered shyly, 'It's so warm in here.'

My heart raced. 'Would you care to go out into the fresh air?' I asked politely and squeezed her hand.

'I'd love to,' she murmured.

I could have jumped the height of the roof.

***

I could see a few hotshots eyeing me with envy as we headed towards the door, and I felt two inches taller. The nonchalant swagger was a mistake, because I stumbled on the step. But I composed myself, slipped my hand protectively around her waist and we stepped into the cold of the night. I remember every detail of that night: A few couples stood nearby, there was a low murmur of voices; a car moved off and its lights faded when it rounded a distant corner. We walked a short distance and stopped at the roadside beside a clump of trees. In the darkness we clung together, swayed gently and our lips met in a long, lingering kiss.

'I haven't seen you here before,' she whispered.

'No. It's my first time.'

'I thought you were never going to ask me to dance,' she said.

'I wanted to practice my dancing first, to impress you.'

'To give me a night to remember,' she replied with a giggle, and her warm lips met mine. The moon faded behind a dark cloud and I felt a cold chill. Her lips moved down my neck and lingered, her body tensed and she gave a low moan. I closed my eyes and thought, *God, she's really fallen for me.*

The moon slipped from the clutches of the cloud and brightness flooded the countryside. I opened my eyes and she looked up. It was her eyes that stunned me – the glazed, burning-yellow look was weird, but worst of all were the white fangs that protruded from her delicate lips. In that instant, some primitive survival instinct quelled my fear and I thrust her away with all my strength. She landed against an old fence post that shattered with the force and she fell to the ground, covered in sharp splinters. In those seconds, scenes from horror films flashed through my mind. It was now or never. There was no other way.

Christ help me, I thought, and grabbed a piece of the splintered post. I raised it high and used a burst of energy and fear to drive it through the red blouse, deep into her heart. There was an instant, acrid odour of sulphur, and this creature or thing began to shrivel and fade. Then, as if ordained by some evil force, once more the moon was shrouded by a dark cloud and a cold, ominous darkness closed over the land. There was a chilling shriek and a haunting cry, like a wolf. In seconds the moon edged clear and in the brightness I gasped in amazement. All that lay at my feet was a splintered post and a pair of black velvet shoes.

In that moment of panic, I grabbed the shattered post and threw it over the ditch. I still don't know why, but I lifted the shoes carefully. They reeked of a vaguely familiar smell: cow dung, I soon realized. In disgust I flung them into the trees and turned quickly, drawn like a moth towards the light from the open door.

My heart was thumping but there was no looking back, and every step was distancing me from the horror of the moment. I was breathing fast. *Slow down, take it easy*, I warned myself, conscious that there were no curious onlookers so far, despite the piercing cry. It had all happened so quickly and the noise had not attracted attention. My movements were a bit slower now, more relaxed, but despite this, I stumbled again on the step at the welcome doorway.

In the cloakroom I was afraid to even glance at my throat. My hand searched for the place where she placed her lips, and maybe her dreaded fangs. A quick wipe of my sleeve cleared the condensation off the faded mirror and I stared in disbelief at a pale, ghost-like figure. *Did I appear different?* My fingers moved across my throat, holding my breath – I peered closer and recoiled in horror. Christ help me, it was plain to see - two faint red marks and a streak of blood. Then, almost afraid to look, I gazed into the mirror and bared my teeth but there was no sign of fangs. Suddenly the toilet door creaked and someone walked to the urinal. He began to hum "Bad Moon Rising" as he bailed the boat. A chill ran down my spine despite being a Creedence fan.

I reached to turn on the cold water. With hand outstretched and trembling, I noticed the prick on my finger and thought of the splintered post. With a sigh of relief, I murmured, 'Thank God,' and washed the blood off my neck. Now I could see that the red marks were nearly gone; so much had happened in a short space of time. My mind was in a whirl, but the sudden urge for a cold drink drove me back to the dance floor, where small groups of revellers still mingled, enjoying the night and reluctant to bring it to an end. I felt distant, excluded, almost in a trance as I walked towards the tiny bar where the crowd had thinned out.

***

The drink was cool and soothing. In those moments I began to relax, enjoying the feeling of security and gradually distancing myself from the horror outside. Everything was so normal that I could almost believe that it was all a figment of my fertile imagination. I silently swore that I was finished with books about the dark arts, and horror films were now definitely taboo. My eyes drifted lazily around the hall but stopped near the door, and I gasped, nearly choking on the Cidona. It was a black-haired girl with a red blouse that clung to her slim figure The blood froze in my veins and my hand gripped the counter. *Maybe it was a twin sister.* Then my eyes moved down her body and I stared in disbelief. She was in her bare feet.

'Jesus Christ,' I murmured and gave a start at a sudden nudge in my side. Mickey Gallagher's voice rang in my ear, 'Are you saying a prayer, chief? You sly old devil – you must have sinned badly. Where's she from?'

Still in a daze, I leaned against the counter for support and lied, 'Through the Gap. Around Lifford or Strabane, I think.'

'Are you meeting her again, huh?'

'You never know,' I heard myself murmuring, being instantly surprised and shocked at my own words. It was utter madness I knew, but I couldn't take my eyes off her. For a moment she glanced in my direction. I thought I saw the faintest hint of a smile, and then she gave an alluring flick of her black hair, turned with a delicate sway of her hips, and walked off into the darkness.

Mickey looked around the hall and nodded towards the musicians who were packing their gear.

'Tell me, what do you think of this wee spot? It's deadly, isn't it?'

I clung to the counter and searched for words.

'It's deadly, all right,' I said, but my eyes were still glued to the open doorway and scanning the darkness outside.

Hawaiian Princess
Marie Hannigan

A plane crashed on the side of Crownarad during World War Two. The pilot lost his way and ended up on the west coast of Ireland instead of wherever he was meant to be. Maybe there was fog. You find that a lot along the coast: mist rising off the cold Atlantic waters from the heat of a summer's morning.

That's why we were here, on Crownarad, that crash. Loni's grandfather was one of the airmen on the plane. Loni knew him only from photographs and her grandmother's memories of her young husband.

There was no fog the day we climbed to the summit to scatter the grandmother's ashes. It was sunny, clear enough to see the scar that the crash had gouged into the hill. You look up and the ridge of the mountain seems as sharp as the blade of a knife, but we came to a flat space at the summit, room for maybe two dozen people at a squeeze. I'd pulled into the centre of that space, scared for my life if I ventured near the edge that the breeze would send me flying over the edge. Anya, I was thinking, you're too young to die, your life, your real life is about to begin. I hunched down to lower my centre of gravity. The others were gazing down at the scar on the mountain. When I saw what was about to happen they were too far out of reach for me to do anything.

And it hit me at that moment, even as I heard the voice calling out a warning: This trip had been a terrible mistake.

***

The tour was for my dad, though he didn't know it. A way to ease him back on the scene. This would be our last holiday together, next year I'd be off on a J-1 student visa. He was adamant that I should go on one of those post-exam trips with my mates, until I told him they'd booked a cheap break to the place where there'd been all that trouble the previous year. In truth, they were heading for Magaluf. Boys, booze and beach. Time for all that once I got to college. I was ready. I wasn't so sure about my father.

For seven years he'd been a stay-at-home dad because, to his mind, the loss of one parent was enough for a kid to handle. His partner in Joe's Place was left to run the restaurant, a job my father loved, while he took on the boring bookkeeping stuff. This was a man who would twirl my mum around the kitchen floor at the riff of a chord. I couldn't remember the last time he'd been out to a music session.

He had put his life on hold for long enough. It was time for me to even the balance.

The poster in the travel agents looked promising, a bus tour with stops at hotels offering retro dancing nights. My dad would rediscover his passion for life and maybe meet a nice companion. Let's face it, there were always more women than men at these things. And Dad was in pretty good shape for his age.

I wasn't far wrong. There were loads of women on the trip and those pensioners had moves. You should have seen them, out on the floor every night. Jiving. Set dancing. Not that I wanted him hooking up with some young thing, but I'd hoped for someone a few decades younger than my granny. There were elderly couples too, venturing out for the old-time waltz. My dad would watch them toddle around the floor and I could see the loneliness on him. I gave up on the retro nights.

See those selfies of us, all those breathtaking sunsets over ocean cliffs – don't they get a bit samey after a while? By the second week I was gagging for a whiff of urban decay. The girls were posting super-cool pics from Magaluf. I told myself it's never as much fun as it looks in the snaps. Still, it looked mighty good.

***

We got to Glen, the last location on the tour. First item up was a walk along the strand. You could see the wind blowing from the swirl of sand across the beach.

Old ladies squealed as it blew into our faces and though I squeezed my eyes shut I could feel hard grit beneath my eyelids. By evening my eyes were watering so hard, I had to take out the contacts and resort to my specs. But there was music rocking out of a little pub, the stuff my dad loves. The place was alive with Irish language students and trad musicians jamming up a storm. And I saw this guy across the room. It was Davey. He had this floppy hair and a tan he got somewhere sunnier than Magaluf. Still, I could tell he was local from the way people went over to welcome him home. We kept sneaking looks at each other. Every time I caught him, he stared down into his pint. The shy type. I liked that.

My dad saw me slipping my glasses in my pocket and grinned. Before I could stop him he had steered me through the crowd to where Davey and his mate were sitting. The pal moved over to make room for us. This was Ash, the Londoner, a guy who could speak without drawing breath. If there's one thing I couldn't abide it was someone who talked more than me. This Ash guy went on and on about their travels around Australia, and how they were planning a trip to visit his aunties and uncles and cousins in the Punjab. Davey was quiet. The chatterbox wasn't giving him space to speak, no chance for him to ask me for a moonlit walk or whatever else he might have in mind.

Come closing time, the Londoner was still going on about Oz, and how the lads had to travel all the way to Darwin before they met any First Nation people.

And when they did run into some genuine Bushmen, how friendly they were once they heard that Davey was from Donegal. Turned out these guys were mad into Daniel O'Donnell and Ash couldn't wait to get to meet this *legend*.

'He ha-hasn't heard Daniel's music yet,' Davey said as the Londoner paused to drain his Guinness.

He was nervous. I took it as encouragement, a sign of the adrenalin rush you get when you meet someone new. My heart was hammering too.

Dad pointed out that Daniel lived at the other end of the county.

'Duty first. We're stopping a few nights 'ere with Davey's mum.'

'I was ho-homesick.'

That's when I figured out why the Londoner always answered for both of them.

'Only natural, innit, missing your mum?'

'Not to mention the aunties and cousins in the Punjab.' I get sarky whenever I'm annoyed.

'Nah, ain't met them yet.'

That Ash, he just had to get the last word in. How would I ever get a shift off Davey if I couldn't get more than two words out of him?

'There's music in the pub every night,' Dad said as we made our way to the B&B. 'You'll see him again.'

***

The next night in the bar, there was no sign of Davey

or his boring sidekick. The barman saw us looking around and maybe he had heard us talking about Daniel. He mentioned the name of a big country star and pointed us in the direction of a small inner bar. My dad's eyes popped, because this guy, this international superstar, really *was* a legend to him.

The sight that met us inside sent an outbreak of prickles all over my skin. Davey and Ash were squeezed into this table with Mister Megastar, who was deep in conversation with two women. Ash had his elbows on the table listening to them, or rather to the one who was doing all the talking. I felt a moment of satisfaction that chatterbox had met his match. Then I saw her. Not the woman who was talking, but the one resting back a little, hands folded, smiling. I could barely breathe. The mad, black, crinkly hair, the rosy complexion, the broad cheekbones.

'Dad, doesn't she look like–'

'Not really,' he said.

Okay, so I wasn't wearing my glasses and everything was blurry. But how did he know I was talking about Mum, the woman he called his Hawaiian Princess?

The singer saw my father hovering. He stood to shake hands with a grin of relief, signed a beer mat and made his escape. The woman - the talker - glared at my father. Then her glance fell on his bare ring finger. Since the time it kept slipping off, that time he lost all the weight, he wore the gold band on a chain around his neck along with Mum's wedding ring. I guess that helped him feel close to her - seven years on that wasn't exactly healthy. I was pleased when Carmella - the motormouth - introduced herself and Loni.

My father returned the courtesy. Once Carmella discovered that I was his daughter, she indicated the autograph. 'And your wife - is she not a fan?'

The look on Dad's face answered that one. In a flash Carmella was leaning into him, all sympathy. She was only too familiar with tragedy, she said. And Loni, too. That's why they were here, to honour a grandmother's dying wish. There was a story there, but we didn't get to hear it. Carmella moved on to how she'd seen Loni's post on the Crownarad website, an invitation to relatives of the crash victims who might wish to join her in a quiet memorial service.

Carmella had reached out, as she put it. She arranged to meet Loni off her flight and in the short time since that meeting they'd become *dear friends*. Carmella had no connection to the air crash, only her own experience of that tragic spot. She gave Loni this brave little smile.

'This woman has been such a comfort to me.'

Carmella looked down at her hands, waiting for someone to ask the question. There was something so false about this, I was about to change the subject. Ash got in ahead of me.

'Wot 'appened to you?'

There was another long pause before she spoke about a school trip that ended in tragedy. A fellow student who'd fallen and been fatally injured. 'I've had flashbacks ever since. And the nightmares ...'

Ash slowly put down his pint. 'That's terrible. But why would you want to come here?'

'Guilt, I suppose. I had to return and ... and apologise to her spirit.'

'Guilt?' Ash asked the question on all of our minds.

Out came this story of a young girl bullied by two classmates. The tormenting and messing had gone on throughout the trip, and Carmella thought it was more of the same when one of the girls screamed at her to run for help.

'So I turned away. But it wasn't a trick this time. And by the time they airlifted her out of there ...'

She burst into tears. And Loni put an arm around her. And the lads were all embarrassed. And Dad asked if there was anything he could do, and she whispered that a little brandy might help. No sooner had he brought the drink to Carmella, than she threw her arms around him in another fit of sobbing. Being a nice guy he didn't pull away.

Later he confessed that it felt as if he'd embraced another woman in front of my mother. So he had noticed the resemblance in Loni though he didn't admit it at the time, because even that recognition felt like disloyalty.

***

What I remember about Mum is her softness and her

smile. My father once told me that no matter who or what they were, people felt at ease with her. She had that knack, he said, because of the still way she held herself, and that smile that seemed to take in the whole world. Unconditional acceptance, he called it. Maybe that was what I saw or sensed in Loni. There was nothing hard or sharp about her. I might have put it down to my fuzzy eyesight, except for the fact that I couldn't see the same warm glow around Carmella. Quite the opposite. There was something jagged about the woman. Something not quite right about her story: Where were the teachers when that school tragedy happened? Where were the other students?

She had killed the mood and any slim chance of my finding a nice woman for my dad. There were two days left, only two days before the tour bus dropped us back to real life. My spirits took a nosedive as we stood to leave the pub. That was when my dad turned to the lads. We were going on a boat trip the next day; would they like to come along? Davey smiled and Ash reacted with predictable enthusiasm. And guess who jumped on the bandwagon?

***

I won't describe the soaring cliffs, or the sea caves, or the pod of dolphins playing in the harbour. I slept through all that, thanks to the travel sickness pills I'd taken before breakfast.

They hit me right at the start of the trip. I was so

spaced out I had to throw myself down on the raised square that took up most of the deck. At one point we must have hit a big wave. I felt the boat heave and woke to find Loni's hands reaching out to support me, her jacket tucked around my legs. I asked where my dad was. Loni pointed to the little wheelhouse: Carmella was feeling sick and had gone inside with the skipper. I could just picture the way she would have fastened her hand in the crook of Dad's arm, obliging him to go in with her. From where we sat I could see her laughing and chatting to the men.

She had rushed to meet us on the pier that morning. Sense had won over vanity and I'd put on my glasses. She was nicer looking than I expected, but just as sharp with her starved-model cheekbones. And while Loni didn't match the photograph in my head, the sense of comfort I felt in her presence was still there.

It came over me then as she smiled down at me, a feeling more powerful than my annoyance at Carmella. I thanked her and said I was sorry about her granny.

'Grandma had come to the end of a very long life.'

I did the sums: If Loni's mum was a baby seventy years ago, the granny must have been at least eighty-eight.

'Does that make it easier?'

'She believed that Grandpa would be there to meet her. That is a comfort.'

Loni had a daughter my age. I discovered.

Madison would have come on this trip but she'd broken her leg in a skiing accident. At the mention of Madison – Loni's daughter was a champion skier – her face lit up with the same cheesy look that my dad got when he boasted about me. They were close, especially since Madison's dad had remarried. She looked away and I squeezed her hand. It was fine, she said, turning that calm smile on me. She'd come to terms with the new wife and they were all friends now.

This seemed like the time to put in a good word for my dad, only the pills were starting to kick in again. Before drifting off I managed to mumble a request.

'Of course,' she said. 'We'd love for you to come with us.'

***

What possessed me? That's what I was asking myself as I struggled up Crownarad the next morning. Ash led the way. He'd insisted on carrying the urn and Loni was sticking close to him for fear he might drop his precious cargo. Carmella was dragging out of my father's arm, chattering away. He kept looking around to check on me. I was trailing behind and Davey fell back from the others, waiting to help me over a stream.

Loni and Ash paused and bowed their heads. They had come to a memorial cairn that people had built to mark the spot of the impact. We hurried to join them and as we moved to stand with Loni, the sniffles started. Carmella. This, I realised, was why I'd volunteered to make the pilgrimage: the thought of Loni all alone in this moment with no space to grieve, because it had to be all about one person. Carmella and her so-called guilty conscience.

'Is that wind rising?' a small voice asked.

The locals had warned that it was breezy up there on the calmest day. Ash looked to Loni and she nodded. She was ready to continue the ascent.

***

The world was spinning. Crouched on hands and knees, I urged my father to stay with Loni. I was fine, I assured him, just taking a breather. Davey hunkered beside me. We watched Loni scattering the ashes. The others were huddled around her and my father laid a comforting hand on her shoulder. Just then I caught the look on Carmella's face. She reversed a few steps to stand behind Loni. Davey must have seen that movement too. He jumped to his feet.

'Carmella, step away.' His voice was calm but strong enough to carry over the wind.

Carmella's head turned. 'What?' She blinked a few times. 'What's happening?'

'You're all standing to close to the edge. You need to move in.' The words flowed smoothly out of Davey's mouth.

Since then I've discovered that Davey's not like other people. He goes calm in a crisis and that serenity helps him to forget himself.

He stepped forward with an outreached hand, and Carmella allowed him to draw her to him.

'What's the panic? I'm fine.'

Ash laughed. 'We're all fine, mate.'

But Dad's arm had gone around Loni's waist. He kept it there too, his free arm linked into mine, until we made it safely down to the road.

****

Fate spins on the breath of a moment and as it turned out, it wasn't the worst ever holiday. To this day my father maintains that Carmella was a perfectly nice woman. I'd taken against her, he believes, because my mind was set on a different match for him. For a time it was a running joke between us, that he managed to get there without my overactive imagination. I never told him that I'd Googled Carmella Mitchelton. There was only one person of the name that I could find and she's deceased. A tragic accident witnessed by an unnamed schoolgirl.

It would bother him, I know, because the thought of her still bothers me, that schoolgirl who'd assumed the name of her victim.

Resurrection

Clarrie Pringle

Frank drove slowly up the hill, rolling the car gently to a stop on the brow. Nearly there now. Needed to prepare himself. No turning back. He glanced in the rear-view mirror, smiled ruefully. Empty road, neither man nor beast. Some things never change. Time had not made a difference to traffic here. He wondered about other things. He took a deep breath, put his foot lightly on the accelerator, topped the hill and braked to a stop.

His chest tightened as his eyes focussed through the windscreen on the panorama below ... heartbreakingly familiar, mind-blowing in its beauty. And the silence. How could he have forgotten the silence? Not even a whisper of a breeze today. In the distance the blue Atlantic met the silver expanse of sky. Truly the edge of the world. A distant village and townlands dotted a landscape glowing greens and browns. The valley unfolded in front of him down to the coast, gushing streams and wee waterfalls sparkling like diamonds on the way. This was the spot where he had paused and turned to take a last look all those years ago, determined he would never see it again.

Now Frank studied the scene before him.

Looked like a few new houses might have sprouted here and there on the river bed. No spires, thank God, like the one that now dominates O'Connell Street, dubbed The Spike by the locals. From the talk he had heard in the bars of New York he had expected myriad atrocities to have been replicated all over the country by the rabid Celtic Tiger during its last, drawn-out gasp. He couldn't see the pier and the village from this angle. Had the Tiger left his mark there? He hoped not.

He sat back and closed his eyes, muscles relaxing after the long hours driving. Five minutes later he straightened, turned the key, anxious now to complete his mission. He was done with the past. Or was he deluding himself? Time would tell!

***

The seagulls woke him next morning, though it was a few minutes before he identified the sound. Frank smiled as he looked round the room. He could see the cracks of light at the sides of the heavy curtains. Daylight - so soon. He stretched, flexing his muscles. The trip had left him tired.

When he'd reached the town the night before, exhaustion and the late hour had banished his desire to explore. He checked into the hotel and silently took to his bed, hoping sleep would rid him of his uneasiness as well as the jet lag.

God, how could morning have come so fast? He groaned as he left the comfort of the duvet and walked to the window – would he be disappointed? He pulled the curtains.

The gulls were circling the pier, ever hopeful. Half a dozen boats tied up – a couple more heading in past the lighthouse. The gulls were in luck, hovering in hope. Not much else astir for past eight in the morning.

There were a few teenagers strolling towards the school out the road, reluctantly forcing their steps. He squirmed, remembering his own feelings. The shouting and whooping would come later in the day after their release from confinement.

He noticed two cars stopped parallel, each facing opposite ways in the middle of the road, windows down, drivers chatting. Frank laughed. He had forgotten the local practice of stopping in the middle of the road for a leisurely chat or to share a bit of gossip. Other drivers would wait patiently. Only a tourist would dare to interrupt with a beep of the horn, unaware they were prolonging their wait by this display of bad manners.

Opening the window, he settled himself comfortably to watch the town come to life, enjoying the dominant position of the hundred-year-old hotel. Frank wondered how long the huge 'Hotel For Sale' signs would remain on show.

He was surprised how the indifference to his home place, carefully nurtured in his busy New York life, seemed to be melting rapidly to a warm recognition of his roots, roots he had not acknowledged in all his years of exile. The anger he carried with him had been put to good use – channelled into work on the building sites of London and later, across the Atlantic, where he found the streets were indeed paved with gold. It was a plus being Irish in New York then, doors opened, opportunities abounded. He concentrated on making money, became consumed by ambition. The irony of his own rejected past being advantageous to forging a future amused him. Money could be his armour, could make him invincible.

Working with contractors on big jobs, eventual promotion to supervising sites, tendering for projects himself, gave him an entrée to the property market. He learned fast, made his name with the contractors and developers – many of them Irish Americans or other Europeans. By the time he was thirty he had expanded the business to include his own property management company. He was then ready to make some modest acquisitions ... which eventually became his most important asset.

Sally had come in to his life over a year ago, at a business meeting no less. Jet-black hair, huge, green eyes and a great smile. He was surprised at the jumble of emotions he felt as he tried to concentrate on her proposal. The details didn't register but he agreed to everything, knowing it would guarantee a future connection with this woman.

A small flame had been lit within him that glowed steadily whenever Sally was around. She had taken him by surprise and he resisted … initially. However, in time his detachment melted. He allowed himself to relax with Sally, learned to trust her. It was strange and scary, but pretty great, to let his defences down, to have someone close to him, warm and loving. His fear of letting someone inside the barriers he had erected in his childhood gradually disappeared. Importantly for Frank, Sally had a mind of her own. Within a few months he was feeling for the first time what it was to love and be loved. It was Sally who gave him the desire and the courage to find himself – insisting as time passed that he must return to his home to complete his journey, become whole again. Lay the ghosts.

****

Reluctantly he left his vantage point. Frank was ready now. No point in further procrastination. He would finish what he set out to do. The walk would be good. Shower, shave – carefully, didn't want any blemishes, needed to make a good impression. No jeans today. Shirt – no, he wouldn't do a tie, that would be going too far. Yes, he looked good in the steam-wiped mirror. Could nearly pass for a real Yank!

He put his jacket on. No need to tempt fate. He knew from experience that bare arms would surely bring the rain. Memories of getting drenched to the skin en route to school, church and dances made him careful. In his teens it always seemed to be raining, though he knew the sun must have been shining sometimes and it was he who walked in darkness. Frank shook himself, shedding the past, walked back and closed the window, just in case the rain came.

***

Leaving the anonymity of the hotel he paused on the steps for a moment – would he recognise anyone? Or be recognised? He looked around him. Not many on the street this midweek morning. Too early yet, only ten. An ancient tractor drove slowly by, the driver acknowledging him with a nod, and a lift of the hand. Frank smiled, remembering how everyone saluted each other on rural streets and lanes. Didn't matter if you knew them or not. It was polite. He had missed that in the cities the first year or two. He worked to acquire the detachment, eyes averted to avoid contact, no acknowledgment of fellow humans.

Walking down the street, he was surprised to see a few of the older emporiums replaced. He had always assumed they would be part of the town forever. The hardware shop was now a fancy boutique, a gift shop replaced the old fishing tackle, and even a beauty salon yelled its miracles for sale on Main Street. Lots more cars too – and a nearly empty car park in the Diamond. He slowed his pace, hands pocketed, whistling quietly. Surprisingly, he was enjoying this trip down memory lane.

As he neared the Corner House pub he stood still in shock. 'Ould Phonsie' was holding up the wall beside the door! Christ, Frank thought, he was old when I was a baby; he must be over a hundred now.

He walked over to him, his childhood friend, a smile beginning. But when he stood beside him, he was careful not to crowd his space. Phonsie had a big toothless grin on his stubbled face. As always he was hopping up and down, the untied laces on his hobnails flapping dangerously. Hands were loosely hidden in the long sleeves of his huge overcoat, which looked like the same coat, too, Frank thought. The blue eyes still danced in the grizzly head, topped by the familiar huge black cowboy hat.

'Good morning to you, Sir.' The hopping increased. 'Are you well?'

Frank laughed out loud. 'Very well, thank you. And you?'

'Perfectly fine, thank you. My health is good today.' He stuck out his hand.

Frank took it, palming the twenty gently into his hand before shaking it firmly, then smiled and passed on, leaving him to his hopping. The bold Phonsie would greet every passer-by similarly throughout the day. Frank smiled at the recollection of the childhood ritual of the daily handshake. Twenty-five years had made no difference.

He had asked his mother once why Phonsie was permanently on the street only to be told: 'Arrah, sure he's grand, he's doing no harm. It's just with him the lift doesn't go all the way to the top.'

This had been yet another mystery to Frank, sure there wasn't a lift to be seen in the village or even in the big town ten miles away – only sometimes in the Hollywood pictures in the hall.

The Diamond and the Main Street were behind him now. He turned down the side road towards the sea and the hills. His mood changed. Muscles tightened, stomach knotted. What would be waiting for him?

***

Fifteen minutes later Frank turned up the lane, noting the hedges had been recently trimmed, the golden gorse tamed, loads of blackberries, still green. Good year for jam! Rounding the bend, his pulse sped as he saw his home for the first time in twenty-five years. He gasped .... stopped ... 'Jesus.' The word came unbidden as he plonked himself on the stone wall. He squeezed his eyes shut, shook his head slowly and opened them again.

His mind hurtled back to his national school days. The five-, six-year-old child, joyful to be getting close to home with stories to tell, reaching safety and love within those walls. And now, just like then, the welcoming door wide open, the bright red geraniums overflowing the flowerpots. The old scene faded slowly, and with it the happy anticipation. He sat until the snowstorm of memories melted in his head and his tightly controlled detachment returned.

A twitch of the curtain at the kitchen window alerted him to a presence. As Frank stood, a figure appeared, hesitated momentarily, then stepped forward into the sunlit door frame. The man put his hand to the side of the door, leaning his weight, steadying himself. Finally, he turned his eyes to focus on the stranger. A frown appeared, back stiffened. Silence.

Frank stared back, lips firmly sealed, eyes hostile. A cat appeared, rubbing his black, furry body against the man's shabby trousers, miaowing softly. The man raised a hand to shade his squinting eyes from the sun.

'Do I know you?' His voice was gravelly, ready for anger.

'You should.'

'I hope I do.' He scratched his chin, puzzled. 'You belong here, don't you?'

'Do I? I don't know. You tell me.'

The old man took a step towards Frank, hesitated, then slowly walked the gap separating them.

Frank could see the tears glinting in the eyes, big drops beginning to roll down the weathered, unshaven cheeks to the trembling lips. Something moved inside him.

'It *is* you.' The words were almost a whisper, unbelieving. 'It is you. Francis. Glory be to God.'

The voice rose on the last words and he lifted both arms, holding them out wide, waiting.

Frank was surprised. He had not expected an embrace … remained immobile, unsmiling. He couldn't do this.

His father let his arms fall slowly to his sides.

Frank put his hand out in a formal gesture. It was taken and held for a few seconds before a gentle shake, the grip tightening as the tears flowed.

'My son, you came back, you are home.'

He beckoned towards the open door.

Frank tried to make a move, but his feet were stuck to the ground. A vision of his mother in her bright crossover apron, arms folded, red hair pinned back from a widely smiling face, filled the entrance. That had been her daily greeting on his return from school. He shook his head, closing his eyes to dispel the image. It represented the only warmth and happiness he had experienced and disappeared when she died in childbirth, baby with her, leaving him alone with a stranger. The man who had made his life hell stretched out his hand and took his elbow, guiding him gently through the door. Inside, little had changed.

Frank straightened and pulled his arm away, scrutinising the kitchen. It was as though he had never left it – not a chair had been moved, everything remained in its proper place, neat and tidy. Same colour on the walls, the picture of the Sacred Heart with the red lamp lit, still scary despite his adult years.

Thoughts came to him of his final day in this room, this house. He walked across to the old chair, ran his hands gently on the curved wooden back.

Frank sat in his mother's armchair, beside the range, the frayed, crocheted patchwork still draped over it. He turned to look at the man who was responsible for his loss.

His father stood silent in the middle of the room. Perhaps he was remembering too? The day when he told the sixteen-year-old Frank to go, go and never come back? Did he know as he spewed the words at him that his son would do just that? There was no mother left to soften the angry words, to comfort yet again the rejected child, embracing him as she explained, 'Daddy doesn't mean it, son, he can't help it, take no notice.'

She had been gone six long years then and her son had had enough.

His father spoke. 'I'll make tea,' he said, crossing to the range to the hissing kettle, pushing it closer to the turf-fuelled heat.

'You make your own tea now?' He realised the stupidity of the question.

'Your mother is long gone, Francis, I've learned to do for myself.' He turned to fill the blackened and dented teapot.

Frank's tension eased as he watched the frailty of this man. His eyes took in the gnarled, bumpy hands, remembering the times those same hands had slammed into his mother's face and body, pummeling her to the floor while he himself took refuge under the table, too terrified to cry out. Not a word was ever exchanged during the batterings, though his mother's tears were accompanied by an occasional moan. When his father was done he would rub his hands together as though washing them before putting each under an arm and mounting the stairs without a word. He could see no sign of this monster in the weak old man before him – where had he gone?

A quiet sob escaped him now and tears started – the memories were vivid and overwhelming. He was angry at his emotion – he had not shed a tear since he left this house. He hid his face in his hands, every nerve end tingling with pain.

'There you are.'

A mug of tea was placed on a stool beside him.

Frank lowered his hands, rearranged his face, his shaking hand reaching for the mug. His father sat in his own big wooden rocking chair at the other side of the range, sipped his tea calmly, eyes gentle now.

Minutes passed.

'I have changed, Francis, I have learned a lot the past years. I am a different man now.'

There was no response.

The old man cleared his throat.

'Are you home to stay, Francis?'

Anger blazed in Frank's eyes.

'This has not been a home since my mother died – you know that.' He looked directly at his father.

'You made it a hard place for her, too. She didn't

deserve that.' His voice trembled with anger.

'You are right, Francis. I will always regret the way I was with the two people who meant most to me in the whole world, son. Your mother knew my history, she never held it against me.' He sighed deeply. 'She was truly a good woman.'

He nodded his head slowly as he spoke the words.

'What do you mean – history? We knew nothing about you, your family, where you came from, anything. When she was alive you hardly spoke, you were like a stranger to me. Same after she was gone.'

'Aye. I was a stranger to myself too then.' His hands clenched and unclenched in his lap, eyes down. 'I knew nothing, and could find no one to tell me anything when I looked. I never had a mother or father, a home … only the nuns and the orphanage. Just pain and hurting.'

His voice faded.

'Orphanage?' There was shock in his voice. His father? No. That couldn't be. Frank had read about them. *His* father? That cruelty and inhumanity?

The old man turned his eyes slowly to look directly at Frank.

'I've hoped and prayed I would see you again, be able to ask you to forgive me.' His voice broke. 'I always loved you. I just didn't know how to show it.'

The tears came again.

Frank wondered if his father was doting. He wasn't making sense. This man was not the cold, cruel father of his childhood.

'What are you talking about now? You can't fool me. I'm moving forward, getting a life. I came back here to lay the ghosts of my childhood, try to figure out why you did what you did to me and my mother. What had I ever done except to be born?'

'You did nothing, son. It was me, I didn't know how to be normal. Your mother was an angel. She tried to show me but I was too scared to let her inside. When you came along it got worse. I was convinced I would lose the two of you if I didn't hang on tight. I knew in my heart I was doing wrong. And then I lost your mother.' He sobbed before continuing. 'I was afraid you would be next ... that was what made me so bad to you. My worst fears were realised when you left.'

He covered his face with his gnarled hands, muttering through sobs.

'I am so, so sorry, my son, I didn't mean to be like that. I have no excuse, none at all. I knew no better.'

Frank was stunned. There was a ring of truth in the words the old man spoke. He felt he could recognise the fear of loss he spoke about.

He rose from the chair.

'I want a normal life for myself. I don't want to be like you. I want to have a real life, happiness.'

He hesitated, then continued. 'I thought working hard, making lots of money would be enough. I thought it would give me a life.' His voice faltered. 'But it didn't. I felt empty inside, there was something missing.'

He walked to the open door and turned.

'I will come back in the morning. I have things to think about. Goodbye for now.'

He did not look back as he walked out.

***

The shore called him. Years ago he had found sanctuary on the boulder-strewn sand, the distant island a deep blue on the grey horizon. As he clambered down the rough, grassy dunes to find his old rock he felt tendrils of life emerging from the darkness inside. Sitting on 'his' rock he allowed a small smile as he felt his adult body fit the shape – just as his childish form had fitted all those years ago. Reflection time.

A couple of hours later, Frank rose. The sea had worked its magic as of old and he had made his decision, calm and unfettered. He looked around him as he left what he, as a teenager, had termed the 'sea of tranquillity'. He would return to it.

Frank took his time strolling back to the town and the hotel, feeling a kinship with the few walkers he met en route. He had phone calls to make, things to do. But first a late lunch in the bar. He smiled warmly at the barman as he gave his order – the laughter and chat of the noisy customers, the sight of kids running about the place filled him with a sense of belonging.

As he turned to pick up the local paper from the counter he was surprised to feel a tap on the back.

'Christ, it is you, Frank, isn't it? My God you haven't changed much in all the years. How are ye doing? Don't you remember me? Johnny Ryan ... we were in the same class.'

'Jesus, I do remember you. Of course.'

That ended his anonymity as Johnny sat beside him, talking non-stop, calling to a couple of others to come over and see who was home at last.

The next morning Frank got some coffee in the supermarket on his way to his house. He was surprised that he was actually looking forward to this encounter. The door stood open and he entered the kitchen to find the old man seated at the table, the sports page of the weekly local spread out before him. He placed a coffee down beside the old man as he folded the paper and straightened his back.

'You came?'

'Yes. And I brought coffee with me - for both of us. You might as well get used to the taste as I only drink coffee nowadays. I won't be changing my habits.'

'Well, I suppose I better have a go. Tasted it once a long time ago. Didn't like it. It was wild bitter.'

He shook his head as he spooned in four sugars and reached for the milk.

Frank waited a while before speaking.

'I've done a lot of thinking since my arrival. I had important things to deal with in my head' He cleared his throat. 'I have spent most of my life alone, working hard. It paid off, made quite a bit of money. I'm a wealthy man. I have decided to change things now.

There is more to life than work.' He put his hand out and touched his father's wrist.

'I talked with someone in New York last night when I left here. We have decided to return to this country, buy the hotel in the town. We'll come home to run it … which means you and I will have an opportunity to get to know each other properly, maybe make up for the past. What do you think?'

His father slowly came round the table, both arms opened wide. This time Frank didn't leave them empty.

'You're coming home, son,' his father whispered as he held him tightly. 'I'll have a second chance.'

'We both will.'

Frank silently thanked Sally for her wisdom.

***

When he phoned Sally later that night he was able to tell her, 'I'm sorted …. you were right.'

He laughed quietly, adding, 'As usual,' before continuing. 'I needed to do this. We'll go with the whole shebang now! You come over to make sure this will be *our* place, we buy the hotel, work together, the whole nine yards.'

There was silence for a minute. Frank's heart filled with fear. Then, her voice …

'Frank, just one question, OK?' She drew a deep breath. 'Total commitment? No doubts?'

'Absolutely. Definitely. Total'.

Frank smiled. He knew she would settle for nothing less.

Neither would he.

Rain

Charlie Garratt

I rose from my chair and peered out of the window. Still raining. Ten days without a break and the drizzle continued to fall from the sky like the Almighty had forgotten to turn off the tap. In the corner Mammy coughed her way through yet another cigarette as she poked away at the fire.

At the bottom of the hill, on the main street, people would be going about their business, wrapped up against the weather and staying close to the shopfronts, seeking shelter. I knew this, though couldn't see them through the fine rain that shrouded everything beyond a few dozen yards, creating stillness and loneliness. Donegal folk are hardy, well used to weeks without a glimmer of sunshine, and we dress accordingly. We get on with what we have to do, because there's no alternative. Everyone knows an infallible forecaster and doesn't hesitate in passing on their knowledge. There's the man from Frosses who keeps chickens and 'is never wrong', or the predictions attached to the brightness of the hawthorn berries, or the RTÉ, or just looking over the hills to see what's heading across the Atlantic in our direction. The simple fact is that if it isn't raining, it will rain sometime soon, and that's the only forecast worth knowing.

'Will I make tea Mammy?'

Another cough, then nothing.

Taking this as agreement, I switched on the kettle before putting teabags into the pot. When I turned to speak again to my mother I saw her slack-jawed and glassy-eyed. This massive, final stroke took her away from me before the teapot had smashed on the floor.

***

It was over a month since Mammy's funeral and I'd been for a couple of pints with Thomas, someone I'd known since national school and now a financial advisor. He'd been friendly enough but kept asking questions about how much I'd inherited, so I suspected he'd only asked me out to sell me one of his investments. Back home it was already going dark and cooler than I'd expected after the fine sunshine earlier in the day. I stepped into my hallway with the quarry-tiled floor and shivered as I closed the door behind me.

Rather than heading straight into the kitchen to pour myself yet another drink I went to the spare bedroom, Mammy's bedroom. The one she'd occupied these last fifteen years since Da died and she'd had her first stroke. Before her death I'd nursed a notion of one day turning it into my sanctuary with a comfortable chair, bookshelves and a state-of-the-art TV, but now there seemed little point. I had the whole house to myself. The walls would benefit from a fresh coat of paint but I knew that each brushstroke would be like washing away Mammy's memory, a betrayal. So I'd put it off. Several times.

She'd been a good mother in her time, when I needed it, when I was young. Not loving, but competent. In recent years I'd increasingly seen her as a problem. I'd missed out on the phase where my mother was an embarrassment to me as a teenager, partly because she was already elderly and decrepit in my eyes by then. She'd married late in life and was almost sixty when I was only sixteen. Mammy was always there, but somehow distant, occupied too much with her own life to be bothered with a small child.

Instead, my discomfort with her had crept up on me in my thirties. Her smoking, the foul mouth, the way she ate her food and a hundred other little things all made me despise her slightly. I'd avoid bringing my friends home, or even staying in the house when she had her cronies round. As for girlfriends, they were a definite non-starter. Mammy would have insisted on having them round for tea then pumped them with silly questions. On the Saturday night after the funeral I'd thought I might go to the Starlight Club. A meal first, then a few jars and if the evening went well I'd be set up with a woman. It seemed a good plan, except for the feeling that the neighbours might consider it too soon, not respectful of the loss of Mammy. So I didn't bother, still hadn't.

***

The day after we'd buried her, I'd cleared my mother's cheap clothes from her cheap wardrobe and slung them into black bags to be taken out to the field. Nothing worth sending to the charity shop, nothing of sentimental value, and I wanted to burn it all, get it out of my mind and my life forever. Still, the truth be told, it saddened me as I consigned her old dresses and even older shoes to the rubbish pile.

When I'd finished on the wardrobe I'd taken a break. Tea and a chocolate digestive, then checked my emails. Nothing exciting, just more condolences. I'd gone back into the bedroom and started on her dressing table, clearing a whole shelf of Body Shop bottles, presents she'd never used but wouldn't throw away herself. Bright red lipstick, cheap from the market, old costume jewellery and a set of rosary beads. Why on earth she had those I'll never know. She wasn't a Catholic, never had been, and as far as I'm aware had only been in a church about three times in the last twenty years.

Having made a good job of the top, I'd pulled open the first drawer and straightway spotted two items of interest. The first was a ring on a gold chain. It looked like an engagement ring and an old one at that. It wasn't my mother's; hers was in a cardboard box in the living room, along with the other effects returned by the undertaker.

The second item to catch my eye that day had been the bundle of bank books. I'd been in no mood to think about money at that time, so had put them back and forgot about them until chatting to Thomas about my finances.

Now I took them out, removed the band and sat down on the bed to look at them properly. I'd never enquired about her finances because she always had cash when she needed it and her contributions to the household bills appeared when required. I guess I'd always assumed that she had a state pension and perhaps a small company one she'd inherited from Dad. Each of the books was full of entries going back many years, so I searched until I found the latest, looking for the final balance. As I'd expected, I wasn't about to become a rich man overnight from her hidden fortune but there was a lot more than I'd have thought, a little over twenty thousand euros, enough for a decent holiday, a new TV and a 'slush fund' to buy the odd luxury for a few years to come.

I wondered how she'd saved so much and it was only when I ran my eyes up the column of figures I noticed the regularity and similarity of the deposits. Every month, round about the fifteenth, a hundred euros had been paid in. At first I thought this must be her pension but I took her to collect that each week from the post office. She always spent a little on groceries and cigarettes, and kept the remaining cash in her purse until she had enough to be worth taking to the bank. Each time she banked it, the amount would have been different. Could it be Dad's company pension? I worked my way backwards through the bank books, noticing that every three or four years there was a slight increase in the monthly figure. It was always a round number, five or ten euros, so not an interest payment or percentage increase. I passed beyond the date of Dad's death. The monthly in-payment was still there, changing back to punts in the last couple of books, on and on until they ran out twenty years earlier.

I got up from the bed and scrabbled through the top drawer again, looking for any earlier evidence but there was none, nor in any of the other drawers. In the corner of her room was a small, built-in cupboard, intended to be a walk-in wardrobe but now probably just a repository for more of her junk. It was locked.

I tried several of the keys on her bunch until one opened it. There, amongst the old suitcases, broken irons and discarded handbags was a cardboard box full of papers. It took all of my self-discipline to stop from tipping the whole lot out on the bed. Instead, I carried the box to the kitchen and lifted everything onto the table.

There were the usual wedding photos, school reports, letters I'd sent to Mammy from university, and the like. I couldn't help but pause my searching and smile at this treasure chest of memories. Who'd have thought that Mammy would have held on to all of these? Still, she'd never throw anything away so perhaps it wasn't so surprising.

Part way down, beneath some old unused Christmas cards, was a shortbread tin, the sort covered with red tartan and a photo of a piper on the lid. Inside, when my shaking hands wrenched it open, were a further five bank books, and a photograph of a young woman and two men of about the same age. Scrawled on the reverse, in my mother's handwriting, was an address.

***

The street was one I'd walked down many times. Houses on one side and a mix of offices, factory yards and public buildings on the other, culminating with the bank on the corner. I checked the back of the photo and confirmed that the house I wanted was next to the newsagent halfway down the terrace. I drew a deep breath and knocked. A man I'd have guessed to be around fifty, dressed in cardigan and slippers, answered the door after a couple of minutes.

'Morning. Can I help you?'

'This will seem very strange.' I felt my cheeks flush. 'But do you recognise anyone in this photo? I found your address on the back.'

He took it, raised an eyebrow and smiled.

'It's Dad, Tommy Breslin. The one on the left. He

looks about twelve but expect he'd be eighteen. It's outside Doherty's Bar, up on the Diamond. Where did you get it?'

He invited me inside for a coffee and I explained I'd found the photo amongst Mammy's things but didn't mention the bank books. He told me his father had died two years back and he didn't know the woman.

'Pretty, though. Your mother you say? I couldn't be sure but the other feller might be Dad's old boss, Gerry Byrne. He once said they'd been good friends when they were younger. All changed when Byrne came back from England. Dad wouldn't speak to him and wouldn't say why.'

'Any idea where I might find this Gerry Byrne?'

'Last I heard he was in that place up at Glenlee, … St Agatha's'.

***

The nursing home was one of these modern, sprawling buildings with a soulless vibe and an early video of Daniel O'Donnell looped on the giant TV screen in the lounge, with most of the residents sleeping in their chairs in front of it. An Asian care assistant walked me through to a room at the end of a corridor and pushed open the door without knocking, then took herself back to whatever she'd been doing when I had disturbed her morning. A bald man well into his eighties lay in bed, an oxygen mask hissing over his mouth. The eyes flickered and he beckoned me to sit down. I couldn't make out his first words and had to ask him to repeat them. Byrne pulled away his mask.

'You're Marion's son. You're very like her.'

'Are you a friend of hers?'

A cheerless laugh crackled in his throat.

'Not since we were teenagers. How is she?'

'She's dead.' It surprised me how difficult I found it to say those words. I was equally surprised to see tears well up in the old man's eyes.

'So it's over at last.'

I told him I didn't understand, which was the understatement of the decade. He stuffed the breathing apparatus back on and took deep gasps, rubbing his forehead all the time. I asked if I should fetch a nurse but he simply crooked a finger for me to lean in closer.

''Why are you here?'

I lifted the photograph in front of his bloodshot eyes. 'Because of this. Is one of them you?'

He nodded. 'Me on one side, Tommy Breslin on the right, and your mother in the middle.'

He shook his head when I showed him the ring and asked if they'd been engaged.

'Not me. Tommy. That was before.'

'Before what?'

'Before I did what I did to her. The reason I've been sending her money all this time. The reason she packed Tommy in and didn't marry for years after.'

He took half an hour to rasp out the whole story. Two sentences in I was shaking and knew I'd have killed him if he'd been a younger man. Afterwards he closed his eyes and asked me to leave. He didn't need to ask twice.

Two days later I heard that he'd died. He'd been saving his painkillers and swallowed the lot almost before I left the building.

***

There was just me and the manager of the nursing home in the mourning party, and rain dripped from our brollies on to the clay as the priest intoned his final words. When he'd finished, the three of us shook hands and went our separate ways.

Mammy's money, or rather Gerry Byrne's money, had paid for his burial and gravestone. I'd sent off the rest to comply with the notice I'd placed in the Democrat.

Gerry Byrne, *St Agatha's Nursing Home, Glenlee. Now at peace. Removal from the chapel of rest on Wednesday to St Columb's Church, Craigboy for burial at 11am. No flowers. Donations to Craigboy Rape Crisis Centre.*

Fog Giants of the Gap
Darren Gallagher

The trees look like people, standing, watching, as a thick fog reveals only their silhouettes. They're like giants long forgotten, standing there, taking in a world that's unknown to them as cars drive past in both directions. I can only imagine what the stream of white, yellow and red lights curving this way and that would look like to a giant awakened from some ancient slumber.

Both of these colossi stand side by side, unmoving, with another three behind them to their right. It seems to me like they are just staring down, mesmerised by the stream of traffic, me being one of them. They are frightening, but also beautiful. I could just stay here and look at them the rest of the evening.

I turn my attention back to the road as a red glow fills my windshield. Easing on the brakes I gaze up at them. I can't look away.

They stand there slightly hunched over, their big broad shoulders sloping downwards at a steep angle.

They look ragged, and my mind immediately sees huge fur pelts on their backs from some ancient creature long forgotten, to fight the cold autumn air.

As I get closer to the Gap – a stretch of road between two mountains – I am even more amazed by what comes into my vision. The mist rolls down the mountains on both sides, creating a blackness that's eternal, devouring the car lights, one by one. But between the gigantic pillars of stone, a pale blue bursts through the fog, casting different shades of blue and white light as its rays struggle to keep a grasp on the falling evening. I can see each stream of light as it fights against the gloom. There must be a hundred of them, all coming in this direction.

I ease on the brakes and allow the car in front of me to speed ahead. I don't care about the cars behind me. I just want to sit here and look at this, take it all in. It feels like someone has just picked me up and dropped me right in the heart of a movie. It's the only place I've ever seen something like this before, and I really don't want it to end.

But of course, there would have to be an abundance of traffic now, of all days. I drive this road every week, and it's never this busy. The distance between me and the car in front makes no difference to how much I can see of this spectacle, as the headlights coming toward me flood my vision and I have to wait till they pass to see it again. There are too many cars today and the daylight is losing this battle.

I think about pulling over and just watching

them as evening dies, but I can't. I'm already late. Maybe this is what has the giants so mesmerised - maybe it wasn't the stream of coloured lights after all. Maybe they watch the artificial lights day after day, week after week, and now that this beauty is created by the mountains, the fog, and the fading daylight they have chosen to watch. Maybe that's why I can see them today. Maybe as they stand there taking it all in they fail to keep hold of the cloak they wear year round, or maybe the combination of the mist and light breaks open the barrier they use to shield themselves.

I wish I had my camera. But at the same time, I know that if I try to take a picture it wouldn't capture what I'm seeing. I'd need a tripod, long exposure, and the exact settings on at least five other options to get the picture that my eyes already see. By the time it would take to set all that up, the moment would have passed, and it would have spoiled my memory of this beautiful scene. No, this is the only way to see it. To capture it in my mind, a picture for me alone.

I speed up again as I'm almost at the other side of the mountains now. There is no longer anything to see. Whatever void I have just passed through has disappeared. I wish now I had pulled the car over and just sat there looking at it, as the giants were doing. I know I'll never get to see that again. Sure, there will be other amazing sights here, there always are. Barnesmore Gap is such a beautiful piece of our county all year round. There was something special about this one though, something magical, and the giants knew it too.

But now that I know about the giants, I'll be watching out for them every time I drive through the Gap. Maybe I'll see them, maybe I won't, but whenever there's a mist around I'll keep an extra sharp eye out. For I believe it's the mist that breaks their barrier, and when it happens again, I'll be there.

Pilgrims
Sally Neary

The driver was not aware of the trail of black smoke the twenty- year-old bus was leaving in its wake. He had coaxed 'Old Bessie' on a long journey from the most southerly county, Cork, to the most northerly, Donegal, to pick up the returning pilgrims. They had spent three days fasting, living on black tea, dry toast and water, and were only allowed one short night's sleep.

They were required to stay awake on their first night on the island, St Patrick' s Pilgrimage, praying round the 'beds', the grave-like structures that lay next to the cold, bog-brown waters of the lake. No one was allowed footwear, and the rough, uneven ground was never a friend to tender feet. Now seated in the comfort of the bus some drooled on the thought of their first real meal, breaking their seventy-two-hour fast, which was allowed only after midnight. Talk of bacon sandwiches or 'full Irish' wafted around the bus. Others thought about their reasons for doing the pilgrimage: exam success, hopes of meeting a suitable partner or health for a family member. All watched as they left the jurisdiction of the Irish State and entered what some considered foreign territory.

The bunting and fluttering flags which were now in their view did not signal celebration for them. No, they had paid scant enough attention to the televised images of burnt-out cars, petrol bomb-throwing youths or soldiers carrying loaded machine guns. But enough had lodged in their collective consciousness to quieten the muted conversation and strike fear into more than one of the devotees.

'Isn't it shocking to see a foreign flag fluttering over the Irish countryside,' one lady remarked to her companion.

'Tis,' was the reply. 'I'll be glad to get back home and out of here. They don't call it the black north for nothing.'

The words were hardly spoken.

Bang.

'Holy God, what was that?' an elderly lady pilgrim asked.

Silence. The bus stopped dead, right in the middle of the road.

The driver tried to restart his vehicle, but to no avail.

'Looks like we have a small bit of mechanical bother.' The driver understated their position.

'I'll call Cork, let them know. Maybe they can send another bus or throw some light on the trouble,' he said, trying to reassure his passengers.

Audible gasps of near terror were his only response.

A voice came from the middle of the bus: 'I don't like to be stranded here, 'specially at this time of the year when tensions run high round these parts.' The date was the tenth of July and unknown to any of the occupants of the bus the natives from the surrounding hills and farms were making their way down to celebrate their five-hundred-year-old identity. In their thousands they were preparing to leave the United Kingdom and enter the Irish Free State: Rossnowlagh beach, County Donegal, their chosen meeting place for the annual Orange March.

***

Bill had not looked forward to this day. This was to be his first such day without his beloved Dorothy. Usually she'd have the back seat of the jeep filled with flasks, sandwiches, tray bakes and all sorts of tasty morsels.

'We're only goin' for the wan day,' he'd tease her, but he was secretly proud of her domestic skills, her no-nonsense approach to life. In his heart he knew that whatever life threw at them, Dorothy was always at his side.

This year his daughter Linda suggested coming with him. He had protested mildly but he was glad of the company. He felt uncomfortable in his good suit. It had been too tight for him for the past five years. But it was not its ill-fitting that caused his unease; no it was the fact that the last time he wore it was to Dorothy's funeral. He remembered that day, after the service was over, standing in his own kitchen eating food made by the kindness of the neighbours. Mechanically, his hand accepted the sandwiches offered but he wondered how they could turn to sawdust in his mouth. When the house had finally emptied he made his way to the bedroom to change out of his 'Sunday going to Meeting' suit and don his more familiar work-wear. Well, he thought, the cows still needed milking. The silence, broken only by the sound of his own breath and the echo of his footsteps, brought home to him how alone he now was.

It had all gone so fast. It seemed like yesterday he had spied her on the bus going to school in Enniskillen. He spent months staring at the back of her head until one day she turned and smiled. Although he never said as much, Bill felt his life had started on that day.

They married two years after leaving school and Dorothy moved from her parents' house ten miles away and took up the running of the farmhouse, caring for Bill's elderly parents in the process. It was as though she was born for the job. Soothing the elder Mrs Caulfield's aches and pains, sympathising with William Caulfield senior's gradual loss of ability to run the family farm. The birth of their only child confirmed Bill's opinion that he was the luckiest man. Neither the loss of his parents, nor the fact that they failed to produce a son and heir, dimmed this view.

***

'What's that bus doin' in the middle of the road Da?' Linda asked.

'Aye, what is right?' Bill echoed. 'Looks like some of them Papist pilgrims,' he muttered under his breath.

'Catholics, Da, they're called Catholics nowadays,' Linda corrected him.

'I don't care what they are called they're in our road.' Bill parked the jeep in front of the bus and approached the driver.

'Yes sir. Are ye in a wee spot of bother?'

'I think it might be more than a wee bit.' Bill heard the sing-song southern lilt of the driver's accent.

'She was losin' power the whole way up. I thought I'd get her home OK.' The driver continued, 'I'll have to get a replacement bus all the way from Cork and arrange to have this one towed down.'

Bill stuck his hands in his pockets and considered his options. Should he turn back and try to negotiate his route another way, perhaps using one of the unapproved roads that were closed to all traffic during the worst of the Troubles? His thoughts were interrupted by a loud, 'Ahem.' Bill turned to see a man roughly his own age dressed in angler's clothes and waders.

'There is a problem? We are on our way to lunch. We cannot travel the road because of that bus and jeep.

We are now six and a half minutes late,' the speaker said in a strange clipped accent, pointing to his watch.

'Six and a half minutes,' Bill said, studying the man. .

'Ja! We are here since 13.45 and now we are late.'

'You're here since 1345!' Bill was amazed. 'Boys but you're looking rightly for ones here that long. We were always taul the Caulfields came in 1615.'

'Da.' Linda had joined them, unnoticed by her father. 'He means – '

'Hush now daughter, this is man's talk.' Bill reflected Linda had a good heart, just like her mother, but she had a habit of interrupting him at important junctures.

'Yes. My name is Gerhard, by the way. And these are my friends Erich, Horst and Rolf,' he said, pointing to his three companions seated in the car that was parked at the rear of the jeep.

'Pleased to meet ye,' Bill said, and shook the angler's hand. Then lifting his hand he waved at his companions.

'We are fishing in your excellent lakes all morning and we catched five trouts. We are going back to our guest house now to eat them. Mona, the lady in charge, she said be back at one forty five and she will have them cooked. We are now seven and a half minutes late.'

'Boys, that's wild entirely. Seven and a half minutes.' Bill could not understand the four men and their rush. Sure women were great at keeping dinners hot and anyway no one started eating till the men were seated at the table. That was always the way in his house and Dorothy never took so much as a spoonful till he was in from working the farm no matter how late. No, Dorothy saw to it that he was served first. No mistake there.

Gerhard observed the speaker. He saw the kindly, almost sad wisp in his dark eyes; the disobedient hair gelled to one side flying above his bald spot; the red face and the pot belly extending the limits of that ridiculous suit. Gerhard had read that tensions could run high in some parts of Northern Ireland around this time of year. He had organised the trip and he felt responsible for the safe return of his friends.

Another voice sounded. 'Now where's the problem here?'

They had been joined by a young man who had parked his car along the jeep in front of the stranded bus – Sean Boylan, a Garda who was returning to resume duty on his first posting. Although not strictly within his jurisdiction, he recognised the bus's southern number plate and could see the alarmed faces of the occupants. He reflected again that this was not why he had become a Garda. He had joined the force because he felt his physical strength, good sense and people skills would not go amiss in the inner cities struggling with drugs, crime and deprivation. In his wildest dreams he did not think he would be sent to this quiet place; a place surviving on the proceeds of summer pilgrimages. He saw the place itself as a landlocked island forgotten by time and the rest of the world.

Linda had caught sight of the young Garda. She was due to begin college in Belfast the coming autumn and was looking forward to meeting others of the younger generation, like herself. Where she now lived with her father, it was all old – could she say boring – people whose only interest was the land and carrying on a five-hundred-year-old gripe. Certainly no one like this tall, good-looking hunk now standing before her. Sean felt her gaze, blushed slightly and returned it. Later, following too many pints, he told his colleague Garda Paid Flannagan that her eyes were almond-shaped and olive-coloured, or maybe it was olive-shaped and almond-coloured. He didn't know. All he knew was that he had to meet her again.

'Our counterparts on the other side of the border are very helpful these days,' Flannagan offered. 'They'd be able to get her name and address.'

***

Sean was now trying to arrange with the bus driver how to coax the pilgrims off the bus, and move the bus off the road to allow traffic flow again. In the meantime, Bill had established that the anglers were German. This interested him greatly. It had surprised him to find relief from his grief at the sight of a famous German politician.

When Dorothy had died earlier in the year he

felt his heart would break, that the light and joy had left his world forever. Still, he functioned. The cattle needed milking and the demands of the coming seasons dictated his work. He had seen men like him cope with such grief all throughout his life; the only acknowledgement of such deep loss was an occasional nod from another man, a soft 'sorry for your trouble' from the girl who ran the local shop. But the unspoken rule was no one spoke about it, no one mentioned her name in his presence and he never raised the subject. Grief was borne singly and alone. For company in the house he turned on television and was absentmindedly watching Sky News one evening. He nearly dropped his fork. There she was, Angela Merkel! There was something about the jaunty way she turned her head, those restrained jackets, the self-assurance within a man's world that reminded him of Dorothy. From then on he could not miss evening news, afraid of missing Angela and the opportunity to marvel at the resemblance to his lost love.

One night as he shared a half pint with Sammy, his lifelong friend and neighbour, he ventured the question, 'Who would that Angela Merkel remind you of?'

Sammy, who was never known for the sharpest eyes, screwed his up to the television and said, 'Tell ye the truth, she has a fierce likeness to your Dorothy.'

That satisfied Bill. He finished his half pint and turned his face to his home with lightness in his chest he had not felt for months. Now here he was standing close to a man from Germany, and he had to ask: 'By any chance would you know that woman by the name of Angela Merkel?'

'Ja, ja,' came the reply.

'Boys oh boys, that is a good one.' Bill stared at the lucky man.

'Da, Da,' Linda was whispering. 'He doesn't mean … never mind, Da.' She too had seen the resemblance of Mrs Merkel to her mother and she did not want to take away from her father's source of comfort, little and all as it was. Anyway her attention was still on the Garda.

'Perhaps there is some way we can move the bus?' Everyone stared at the speaker, Erich, who was now standing nearby, accompanied by Horst and Rolf.

'Maybe we could …?' Rolf made pushing gestures with his outstretched hands.

'Aye, good man. Up there for thinking,' Bill said, pointing to his own head. 'I have a piece of good strong rope used for pullin' calves.' Bill referred to the common obstetric procedure for birthing cows. 'I could tie it round the front of thon bus and try and pull her with the jeep.'

'It would help if some strong men got behind and pushed, just a small push would get it to the side,' Rolf suggested.

Then, addressing the driver, he said, 'Sir. We will move your bus by a combination of pulling by the jeep and pushing by the men.'

'Right oh. I'll slip her into neutral,' the driver

agreed.

The pilgrims dismounted the bus; the women clutching their holy medals, plain biscuits and bottles of fizzy water; the men rolling up their sleeves pushed with all their might. The jeep strained under the pressure but finally the old bus rolled safely into the side of the road. A loud yahoo went up and all clapped.

Sean drove onward to his work with one last backward glance at Linda. The anglers resumed their journey to their lunch. The pilgrims contented themselves with hot tea, already rehearsing the story to be told on reaching their Cork homes.

Bill started the jeep again and he and Linda headed to the march in Rossnowlagh. He could not believe he met someone who knew the famous Angela. Linda could not believe she had just met such a stunner of a man in this place above all.

As for the place. In the silence that followed the departure of all the people, it reverted back to its true owners. Unaware of borders, flags, marches or pilgrimages, the mists curled down from the surrounding hills with their invisible army of midges. These had been here for thousands of years and will remain, for they know their own place by its very soul.

Rosie

Ann Garratt

Rosie's face glowed as she beckoned me into her kitchen for a 'wee cup of tea'. I had been for a walk and was heading back to our Donegal holiday cottage when a sharp shower drenched me to the skin. We hadn't met before, but I'd passed her house with its green corrugated roof many times, and had hoped curiosity would get the better of her and she'd introduce herself.

My saviour was a stout woman, her long greasy hair, grey-steaked, escaping from an untidy bun. Her face was large, her features open and generous, with the widest mouth that smiled from ear to ear. I imagined that in her youth she was lovely, for that hint of beauty lingered about her still.

After our first meeting Rosie got into the habit of rapping on her window and offering a cuppa whenever I passed, so that by the end of our holiday I'd come to know her quite well.

***

Her home had its own charm, laden with bits and pieces she'd collected over the years. A white rocking chair left over from the sixties occupied one corner of the room, and a pine dresser filled with ancient crockery leaned against the kitchen wall. Most striking was a large crimson Afghan rug, its edges frayed, covering most of the flagstone floor. A small, blue Formica table sat by the window, where Rosie ate her meals.

For company she kept a couple of cats, and consequently, ginger and black hairs littered every surface. But she loved those moggies, they were like her children. She was on good terms with everyone, and neighbours smiled indulgently when they admitted she was no housekeeper.

As I got to know Rosie I found she had a lifelong reputation as a hard worker. Even in her seventies, when we met, she was still out in all kinds of weather tending the animals. She kept a few cows and a flock of sheep, which she managed with occasional help of a young boy from the town. Neighbours praised her dedication, as year after year she worked, full of energy and enthusiasm. But shortly after we bought our holiday home the price of cattle and sheep collapsed and the farm failed. She took it badly, and soon she barely moved from her seat by the window, smoking Woodbines, drinking tea and petting her cats. She was no cook and existed on soda bread and packet soup. So during my holidays I got into the habit off making an extra dinner for her. She was especially fond of my lamb and barley stew, which she kept on the go for days by adding potatoes. To pass the time she read the Donegal Democrat, cutting out her favourite stories and pasting them into scrapbooks, which she stacked up under the range. Whenever I enquired gently about her past she would clam up, maintaining she had no close relatives, though occasionally she would receive a visit from relations who lived in New Zealand. She had a lovely black and white photograph of them above the fireplace. It was evidently taken sometime in the sixties because the three young men sported Beatle haircuts and tight, shiny suits.

The year before I met Rosie, my mother had passed away in a Coventry nursing home. I'd gone to sort through her belongings when the matron, a tiny, roly-poly woman with twinkling eyes, passed me an envelope.

'Mary said you were to have this, and was most adamant. She hoped you'd understand.' She smiled sympathetically.

Since Dad had passed away, Mum had deteriorated. She'd become very demanding and her moods could turn on a sixpence. She complained that staff and other residents were stealing from her, that she was being awakened in the night by laughing and shouting and that men at the home were trying to get off with her. At first I took her complaints seriously.

However, it soon became obvious that a possible explanation was that she was developing dementia. As I slipped the note into my handbag I dreaded to think what it might contain. The process of clearing out the room was more emotional than I'd anticipated. My mother had always been a hoarder so I steeled myself for what I might find. In the chest of drawers beside her bed I came across a bundle of old photographs of me, and underneath a pile of my infant clothes folded neatly. Next to them was a tiny wooden box that I thought at first contained misshapen pearls, but I soon discovered they were my baby teeth. Tears pricked my eyes. I took a deep breath and carried on. Her wardrobe was stuffed with jumpers and skirts, some never worn. Finally at the bottom of a cupboard I happened upon a brown folder with dozens of paintings and drawings I'd done in primary school. Looking through it I felt regret that I had not been more patient with her at the end - certainly I should have humoured her a little more. With dismay I realised my mother had been utterly devoted to me, but I'd been so busy with my own life I'd hardly noticed. Again I shook away tears as I put aside the pieces I wanted to keep and consigned the remainder to black plastic bin bags for my husband, Dan, to take to the charity shop. I was just about to close the door on her room when I remembered the envelope in my bag. I sat on the edge of the bed and opened it.

I couldn't quite grasp the words on the page. My heart was pounding. I must have been in shock.

'You all right, luv?' Dan asked when he returned to collect the bags and saw my ashen face. I handed him the letter, and he scanned it.

'You had no idea?'

I shook my head. He sat down beside me and squeezed my hand.

'How could they?' I stammered, feeling my insides cave in. 'They always said they never knew my birth mother, only that she was Irish. After all this time. Why tell me now? You know that I've often thought about her over the years, but dismissed the idea of trying to trace her for fear of offending them. Then you and I had the kids, so I just put it to one side.'

'It says that she's still alive, and your mum received a Christmas card from her every year. Wow, I can't take it in. Do you recognise the name or the place?'

I shook my head.

'Never heard of her and my parents never mentioned Donegal. Mum says a condition of the adoption was that they swore not to tell me. Why do you think she did it now?'

'I don't know, luv. Guilt? Maybe she just wanted to set the record straight.'

'What shall I do?' I stammered. Dan put his arm around my shoulders and hugged me tight.

'Give yourself time. You've had quite an upset. Let's go home and think about this.'

I felt drained and my legs almost gave way as I

tried to stand. My husband pulled me up and we headed to reception, where we handed the keys of Mum's room back to the matron.

I felt numb.

***

That first time I went to Donegal I was bowled over by the raw beauty of the place, the Bluestack Mountains towering over the landscape and to the west, the white spray of the Atlantic as it crashed against the shore. Surrounded by so much beauty I felt a rush of grief for the life that had been lost to me when I was given away. I had grown up in a high-rise flat in the middle of Birmingham, always longing for something better. Now I asked myself if I would have been happier in rural Donegal, but the reality is my alternative past would most probably have been one of hardship and alienation. I'd have been an illegitimate child, growing up in a Catholic country.

It was Dan's idea to buy the holiday home near my birth mother. We found a small, white, thatched cottage at the bottom of a hill, a stream running though the garden, and fell in love with it. This was our retreat, our gift to ourselves. We visited as often as we could, about four times a year. Every time I arrived I felt a sense of pride that I'd come from such a magical place.

I never told Rosie that I knew about our connection. When I thought about it, I couldn't bring myself to intrude. Anyway, it was more her secret than mine. Thankfully I had a loving relationship with my adoptive mother and I wasn't searching for another. I imagined her years ago, frightened and alone and having to give her baby away. Every time I thought about it, it made me want to weep.

After I met Rosie I used to wonder about my dad. Was he one of the local farmers or had she met a stranger and fallen in love? But I wasn't about to quiz her so I resigned myself to never knowing.

During one holiday in Donegal Rosie confided in me that doctors had told her she had a heart condition and had advised her to take things easy. Occasionally she would complain of feeling tired. She made light of it, but her face would turn grey and she would gasp for breath, so I knew it was serious.

****

After we came home, I was dusting a photograph of my adoptive mother when I thought about Rosie and her heart condition. I made up my mind to tell her the next time we met.

Then one day her heart gave out. She'd been waiting to go into hospital to have a procedure. I was devastated. I felt consumed by regret that I'd never said anything and bitter that I'd only known Rosie for three short years when she was taken from me a second time. We flew over for her funeral. Afterwards a neighbour handed me a battered chocolate box with a faded picture of an Irish cottage on the front.

'I don't know what's in it. The day before she passed away she could hardly breathe but made me promise to give you this.'

I sighed and smiled. 'Probably some press cuttings she was saving.'

***

That night, after Dan had gone to bed, I sat before the turf fire and emptied the contents of the box out onto the table. A strong smell of cigarette smoke rose from the crumpled envelope and the bundle of photographs that spilled out. There was also the cameo broach I had given her two Christmases earlier. She'd worn it every time I'd seen her since then, so she must have put it away in the box just before she died.

I carefully opened the envelope to find a letter, typed on church letterhead. It was dated August 1952 and signed by the parish priest. In the most perfunctory of terms the correspondence gave Rosie details of my adoption, instructing her, on pain of her immortal soul, never to make contact with her child. I was amazed therefore when the cache of photographs turned out to be pictures of me as a baby: my First Holy Communion, me at primary school, as a teenager, at college, my wedding day. Through the photographs my adoptive mother had sent, Rosie had kept hold of a small part of me.

The yellow haze of dawn lit the sky before I

finished reading and rereading the letter and examining the well-thumbed black and white images. I had known Rosie for several years. Why did she never say anything? Maybe feelings of guilt overwhelmed her and she couldn't face me. Perhaps she thought I'd judge her. I sat back on my chair and let out a breath. I was stunned that both of my mothers had chosen to reveal the truth in the same way and only when they faced death.

In the end I placed everything back into the box and put it away. I resigned myself to the fact that I would never hear my birth mother's story, but a part of me longed for her to have looked into my eyes even just once and told me she loved me. As I tried to make sense of my situation it struck me that I wasn't alone. Many people had stories like mine, stories without a fairy tale ending.

***

These days when I'm venturing through the mist, past Rosie's cottage, my step lightens as I remember those special times when I came to know my birth mother. Dan always says he can see something of her in me; my smile and my willingness to roll up my sleeves and get stuck in. I never thought I'd find my mother and she probably never expected to meet her daughter. My life didn't unfold in quite the way it might have – perhaps neither of ours did.

I've been lucky. I've shared the love of two

mothers and it fills me with gratitude, despite the secrets we kept.

The Homework

Malachy Sweeney

Eoghan rooted through a bundle of old newspapers. *These long evenings are a godsend,* he thought.

It was impossible to get time to read during the week, and he always kept a few old issues to browse over, especially when the long, dark evenings arrived. He glanced over a few pages, and eventually it was a faded headline that captured his attention. With the newspaper settled on his lap, he sank into the armchair with a sigh of contentment. He stretched out his legs towards the fire and was soon engrossed in an unusual tale about a mysterious flying object.

'There's no day in it since the time changed,' Kathleen remarked.

There was no response.

'I might as well be talking to myself,' she said quietly, and crossed the room to pull the curtains. At the window she paused to look across the front garden towards the white-capped waves that swept across the bay. In the fading light the bay appeared dark and forbidding. She drew the curtains and the cold, outside world faded, while the open fire cast a warm glow around the room.

***

Seated at her desk near the stairs, Mary was engrossed in homework. She could still hear the English teacher emphasising the importance of revision and the value of good planning. Mary checked her timetable and marked off the science and maths. She enjoyed working out the problems, and anyway Mr. Doyle was so helpful and definitely her favourite teacher. But the English homework was wrecking her head. It was one thing to write when the topic was clear, but tonight it was not. Worse still, she had left the English book in her school locker.

'I want you to do some research, and we'll discuss it tomorrow,' the teacher told them.' Then he wrote a three-word quotation on the whiteboard. A few students asked questions, but the bell had gone and the next class was waiting at the door.

'The quote relates to Romeo and Juliet,' the teacher told the students, as they filed out the door. 'We'll look at it in detail tomorrow.'

Mr. Doyle always emphasised the importance of students' using their initiative, but this was a bit much. She shook her head in frustration. *I really should have looked at this earlier, when my mind was clear.* For a moment she thought of texting her friend Emily, but it was too late.

Perhaps there is still a chance, she thought, and looked towards her mother. There was a note of desperation in her voice.

'Mammy. Do you know anything about Shakespeare?'

Her mother gave a rueful smile and shook her head. 'Child dear, I had to go out into the world when I was your age. There was no Shakespeare for me. Shakespeare wouldn't put bread on the table when I was young.' Kathleen paused for a moment and looked towards the man behind the newspaper. 'Why not ask himself?'

Mary passed no remarks on the reference her mother made to 'himself'. She looked towards her father sitting in the armchair, and could see he was immersed in the old newspaper. *It's curious the way old newspapers always seem more interesting*, she thought, and was reluctant to disturb him. *Anyway, he probably wouldn't know very much about Shakespeare.*

'Mammy – he wouldn't ...'

Her mother raised an eyebrow. 'There's only one way to find out, and you might be surprised.'

'Daddy!'

'Yes love. What is it?' Eoghan asked.

'Shakespeare – did you ever hear of Shakespeare?'

He lowered the newspaper. 'Shakespeare ... is that yer man, Willie Shakespeare?'

Mary smiled. 'William. His name is William.'

Eoghan lay back in the armchair and studied the ceiling. 'Willie Shakespeare,' he mused, as if the name was that of an old friend. 'Wasn't that boyo that said the whole world's a stage?' Without waiting for a reply he began:

'All the world's a stage:
'All the men and women merely players;
'They have their exits and their entrances;
'And one man in his time plays many parts,
'His act being seven ages. At first the infant,
'mewling and puking … and spitting and farting.'

'Daddy!' Mary interrupted. 'There was no spitting and farting.'

Eoghan put his head back and laughed. 'It must have been a different book that I read.'

Mary looked with surprise at her father, so relaxed in the armchair. There was so much she didn't know about the quiet man that read his newspaper in the corner, or her mother who seemed to have such an inner strength and never complained. For a moment she tried to imagine her parents as teenagers, but was drawn back to reality by her mother's voice.

'What did you want to know about that buck Shakespeare anyway?'

'Ah, Mammy. It was just something he wrote.'

'Come on,' her father prompted. 'Let's hear it.'

She hesitated for a moment to get the feel of the words. 'We burn daylight,' she read slowly.

'We burn daylight,' Eoghan repeated. 'That's a good one, all right. Mind you, I often burned the midnight oil, but never daylight. It is a *quare* one, I'll grant you that.'

'You better hurry up or you'll be futtering about all night. Why don't you use that Googly thing you're always on about?' her mother suggested.

'Mammy, it's called Google and I'm not sure that will be much help.'

'Well give it a shot anyway,' her father advised. 'It can't do any harm.'

There was a brief silence that was broken by the low whirr of the computer and the occasional crackle of the logs on the open fire.

Eoghan rustled the newspaper impatiently and said, 'Well?'

'Hang on - just a minute. There … there it is. It says that it has come to mean, wasting time. But it also refers to Romeo and Juliet, and Mercutio.'

'Is that all?' he asked.

'The full quotation is: "Come we burn daylight, ho!"'

Eoghan smiled and looked towards Mary. 'Ho, ho, indeed.'

A loud rap on the door captured their attention. Perhaps inspired by the Shakespearean language, Eoghan called out in a commanding voice, 'Enter.'

The door opened slowly and Seamus Furey stepped out of the darkness. Seamus was a regular visitor but there was a look of surprise on his face.

'Don't mind him, he's just acting the maggot,' Kathleen explained.

'You arrived in time, Seamus. We were just discussing Shakespeare – Willie Shakespeare,' Eoghan said.

'Well, I can tell you one thing for sure,' Seamus responded. 'There was nivir any Shakespeares around this neck of the woods. There was a Willie McCloskey all right, but nivir any Shakespeares.'

'And mind you, it's not a name you'd forget in a hurry,' Eoghan suggested.

'That's for sure,' Seamus agreed.

Seamus rubbed his hands together. 'Do you know what I'm going to tell you, it's sharp enough tonight.'

Eoghan nodded in agreement. It is. It's bitter all right, but I suppose it's that time of the year. Pull up to the fire and warm yourself there.'

Seamus held his hands towards the warmth of the fire. 'Aye! It'd cut you to the bone, right enough.'

***

Mary returned to her homework. She was never sure when her father and Seamus were serious or engaging in light-hearted banter. She decided to surf the web for a few minutes but was still half-listening to the conversation in the background. She opened a few tabs that were of no real interest but then the exchange between Mercutio and Romeo was in front of her. She read it carefully:

Mercutio told Romeo, 'Come we burn daylight, ho!'

Romeo responded, 'Nay, that's not so.'

Mercutio continued, 'I mean, sir, in delay. We waste our lights in vain like lamps by day.'

It was all a bit vague until the accompanying notes revealed that Mercutio was endeavouring to draw Romeo away 'from the mire of all this love nonsense, where he was entrapped up to his ears'.

Mary gave sigh of relief and began to write. She thought she had it now. But the pen faltered and then stopped - her mind was drawn to the next words her father spoke.

'You know, Seamus – the *girseach* was just taking about Romeo and Juliet. Mind you - that brings back a few memories.' He looked towards his wife at the fireside.

'Kathleen! Do you remember the time we were out there - abroad?'

'Indeed I do. It seems like just yesterday,' she replied, and placed a log on the fire. A thin sliver of dry wood blazed brightly and then faded.

'Verona. That's where it was. Verona,' he repeated, as if to refresh his memory. Again he looked at his wife, with the glow of the fire on her face.

Once more, he could see a young girl with her face lit up by golden rays of the sun. That was a time when we were both so young, walking hand in hand down narrow Italian streets that were thronged with elegant people. They all sauntered along as if the day would last forever and the buzz of voices added to the energy. Smaller streets that turned off sharply to the right and left were also filled with people. He could still see it in his mind, like an endless fashion parade.

He nodded. 'Yes. We were there. It was like walking into a different world. We passed this ancient arena where they hold big concerts every year.

'Then we went down this narrow street and there in front of us … it was like bees at a hive, all the people moving in and out through a small archway.' As he spoke, Eoghan swept his hands in the air in the shape of an arch. 'Curiosity got the better of us,' he said. 'We dandered in for a look and couldn't believe what we saw. The walls on both sides of the archway were covered with graffiti.'

'I suppose it was a bit like Belfast,' Eoghan ventured.

'Oh, goodness no. This was so different,' Kathleen said. 'There were names and little drawings of hearts, pierced with arrows. These little love symbols in so many colours. It was like a lovely wallpaper.'

'It must have been powerful,' Seamus remarked.

Kathleen nodded. 'It was, all right. I can still see it, with the writing of all shapes and colours.'

'That's right,' Eoghan agreed. 'We moved with the crowd into a small courtyard, where the walls were covered with more colourful graffiti. There was a small wishing well but no one bothered about it. They were all looking up at a balcony. Young men and women stretched to throw coins up onto that balcony. Sometimes they laughed and kissed when the coins landed. We just stood and watched. We never saw anything like it before. Do you remember that, Kathleen?'

There was the hint of sadness in her voice when she replied. 'I do indeed. I can still see the crowd, so young. Just like ourselves back then.'

'I couldn't figure it out at first, but then I realized why they were throwing coins onto the balcony. You see, we were standing where Romeo stood, when he called up to Juliet. There in that beautiful little courtyard in Verona.' Her voice trailed off.

Mary watched her mother reach for another log and place it on the fire. There was no flicker from the blaze this time; there was only silence and the ticking of the old clock on the wall.

For a few minutes Mary was lost in a vision of the little courtyard filled with young couples, including her parents. She glanced again at her father and mother, who never ceased to surprise her.

Kathleen rattled the teapot. 'You'll have a cup of tea, Seamus.'

'Indeed an' I will. Thank you, missus.'

'And I'll put your name in the pot too,' she said to Eoghan.

'Powerful stuff, isn't it? We burn daylight,' he mused. 'Isn't that a strange way to say something simple? He could have said they were just shooting the breeze. Sure that would do the same job. You and me, Seamus, we'd just say, blathering on about nothing, or "gabbing away," in our real plain English.'

'What was that bit about the daylight?' Seamus asked.

'Oh dammit, I forgot. Sure Mary read that bit before you came in,' Eoghan explained. 'It was yer man Shakespeare that wrote it.'

Seamus shook his head. 'I'm afraid it's a new one on me.'

Eoghan took a sip of his tea and looked towards Mary. 'What did you discover about this whole business anyway?' he asked.

Mary sighed. 'I'm still not sure. But it is something about Mercutio trying to advise Romeo that he should pull back from the mire of all this love nonsense, where he was entrapped up to the waist.'

Seamus savoured the raisins in a piece of rich barm brack, but felt a bit at sea with all this Shakespeare stuff: *Most nights we talk about politics, or how the farming or fishing is faring out, but the Shakespeare talk is a bit rare. Still, it whiles away an hour on a winter's night,* he thought.

'Speaking of trapped, did you hear about Doherty's cow,' Seamus asked.

'Hear about it be damned. Sure wasn't I there.'

'Go to hell.'

'Indeed an' I was, and me nearly up to my waist in the muck trying to get her out. I was damned lucky I wasn't lost myself.'

'And how is the cow faring out?'

'She's well shook, but she'll come 'round.'

'It'd be a big loss, and between me and you...'

***

Mary looked at pictures on Facebook and smiled at the image of Frank Martin, a boy at her school. She thought of her friend Emily singing, "Frankie and Mary are sweethearts…"

'The homework must be finished when you're smiling,' her mother said.

'Ah, it's just something I was thinking about.'

'You don't want to burn the midnight oil,' her father remarked.

Mary closed her book and switched off the computer. *I shall not waste my light in vain or burn the midnight oil,* she thought.

Her father and Seamus were deep in conversation as her mother gave her a goodnight kiss. Mary climbed the stairs, paused at the creaking step and called, 'Goodnight, everyone.'

She smiled when her father called, 'Goodnight, sweet princess.'

***

Mary folded her clothes and placed them on a chair beside the bed. Her pyjamas felt warm and comfortable. She slipped under the bedclothes and snuggled into the soft pillow. Through the large roof light, she gazed at the stars twinkling in the cloudless sky. It had been a long day, and thoughts flooded her mind. There were her friends at school, and Frank, who was so cool – Emily said that everyone thought so

– and then there were her parents, so young at heart. But why did mother seem a little sad? Maybe tomorrow she would ask, and someday soon she too would travel and see those far-off places.

With a sigh of contentment and a feeling of warmth, Mary closed her eyes and was soon floating off to a small courtyard, where young lovers held hands and threw coins on to a decorative balcony, when all the daylight in the world was theirs to burn.

The Bloodstone
Marie Hannigan

It was the night before all that trouble with the seals, and we were sparking off each other like the raw edges of knives. My mother said it was the moon - a blood moon - and its fat, livid face had sprung tides so high they licked across the nose of the pier.

My brother was wired, sleeping all day, on the prowl half the night. I was edgy too, waiting for the *Leviathan* to land, the end of my trip off. When I'd taken the berth, my father had warned that a woman aboard a boat was nothing but trouble. Now that I'd proved him wrong, he was sulking with me.

Kara was like a briar.

She'd been on the warpath since the fishermen held a crisis meeting with my father. Anxious for guidance from their long-time spokesmen, they had come to Stenk, complaining about the poor season, depleted stocks; the infestation of seals on the Inish. My father acknowledged the need for action, and quietly declined to take part. After they had gone, Kara lit on him for not trying to stop them. Stenk uttered just four words.

'People have to live.'

You'd think Kara would have seen the sense of this. Nineteen years old with a child to support, but there are times she acts like a kid herself. By evening, she'd got Radio Annie to launch an appeal on the net: Save our Seals. And away she went to hawk her petition around the pubs. Thursday night. Boat-landing night. The bars would be full of fishermen. To them, the only good seal was a dead seal.

When I told her she'd get nothing but hassle, big brother butted in.

'She can do what she likes.' Typical Manus.

I waited for my father to wise them up. They'd never seen seals tracking a boat, or watched while the little thieves surged up with the nets to bite a live salmon in half. My father said nothing. That bugged me so much, I left the house.

***

Three vodkas on I began to chill out. Perched in the balcony of the Starlight Club, Val was on the prowl. It was almost a year since the last disastrous fling. Funny, how time blurs the worst of memories.

The bar was filling up. My brother came in with a bearded figure: Jackie the Prophet, so named for his biblical appearance and his vast knowledge of mining. It was Jackie's first trip home since the accident that made him a hero in our house. I'd liked the Prophet long before he'd pulled my brother free of a collapsing tunnel. From the first time Manus had brought his gaffer home, I'd hurled my wild desires against the rock of his stillness. The Prophet never seemed to notice.

I turned my attention to a group at the bar, strangers who didn't act like strangers. To a fisherman, any port is home. My focus zoomed in on the tall one with the confident swagger. He caught me watching and smiled. It was enough. One of us would make a move before the night was out.

My line of vision was broken by a pair of bouncers rushing to the scene of a disturbance near the entrance. How small my sister looked, surrounded by wagging fingers. She slipped past the bouncers to offer her petition to the lads at the bar. The tall one turned his back with some throwaway line that prompted an explosion of laughter from his mates. A crude insult - I could tell from the way my sister's head went down. I was relieved when she scuttled for the exit.

I descended to the bar. The tall fisherman caught my waist as I was passing. His eyes were so deep you could dive in and drown in them. I slapped his hand away. My sister might be an idiot, but blood is blood.

Manus was bending Jackie's ear when I squeezed in beside them. My brother was leaning across the table, shouting to be heard above the noise from the disco. The music changed and a couple of cowboy-booted lovelies called to the Prophet to join them on the floor. He stood and I felt a plunge of disappointment, then panic, when he took my elbow. I could wriggle a hip with anyone but that country stuff defied me. By the time the line-dancing section had ended, I was hot and discouraged.

Manus had gone to the bar. I pulled off my sweat-soaked shirt and saw Jackie taking in my skimpy top before averting his eyes. 'Anyone pushing thirty would feel ancient in this place.'

'Thirty next birthday? It's hard to tell with all the fuzz.'

He fingered the beard. 'Even I can't remember what I look like without it.' He sneaked a glance, smiling, and I held on.

The moment was broken by my brother's return with the round.

Jackie stood to go. 'First night home. Jet lag. You know how it is.'

Manus frowned at the untouched drinks. 'You haven't even told me about the job in the States.'

'We'll meet for a yarn tomorrow night,' Jackie said. 'The Beach Hotel about nine?'

The invitation was for Manus. But that was never going to deter this girl.

***

On our way home, Manus put a hand on my shoulder to steady himself. He'd only taken a couple, not enough to leave him legless. That's how he'd been since the accident, two beers and he was gone. He paused to let the vertigo pass, and we stared up at the maze of seagulls tormenting the lights of a boat. *Leviathan* was landing. Manus clocked my grim expression.

'Time to pull on your fishing boots.'

I shook my head. 'Cook never sees the deck. I'm stuck in the galley, peeling spuds. It's not my idea of real fishing.'

'What's real fishing? Gutting fish on an ice-cold deck? No money half the time.' He's still bitter about that hard winter on my father's boat.

'I like to feel the deck beneath my feet,' I said. 'You know that buzz when there's a swell up and you head into a wall of sea? It's not the same on a tank boat. I'm dying of terminal boredom.'

'No man on the scene?'

'Some of us are programmed to go for the wrong kind. Scientists have proved it. They're trying to isolate the rogue genes so they can warn susceptible women.'

Manus laughed, but I knew my own weakness for hard-living men, and the last one had scared me. I didn't tell Manus all this, but he sussed that something had dented my cockiness.

'You should find yourself a decent bloke like Jackie,' he said.

This might have been a general statement, or my brother's way of giving his blessing. It made no difference. Jackie would never make a move on the sister of a friend; it went against some stupid code of honour.

***

We found Kara in a heap on our front doorstep, the petition abandoned at her feet. Manus sat down to console her. Across the street a door flew open and Annie came puffing towards us. She was waving a printout, the response to her internet appeal.

'*Gaia* is coming to monitor the situation. She'll be here Sunday night at the latest.'

'Who the hell is Gaia?' I asked.

'It's not a *who*, Val. *Gaia's* a sailing ship. Belongs to Marine Action.' Annie beamed. 'They'll put a spotlight on the Inish. There will be no seal cull while they're about.'

She was wheezing from her dash across the street. The Ventolin came out. She plonked herself down and sucked on the inhaler. There were three of them blocking the doorway now.

I turned on my heel and made for the boat.

One advantage of being the only woman on a super-trawler - you don't have to share cabin space. I was burrowing under the duvet in my stateroom when it came to me: We'd be going to sea in a couple of days, a six-week trip. Jackie would be gone by the time I got back. I lay awake, planning my strategy until the blood moon gave way to first light.

***

That night, I strolled into the Beach Hotel like it was any other night, though I'd pulled out all the stops. Almost. The flat sandals didn't quite match the plunge-neck dress and red silk camisole. My action plan ruled out the matching six-inch heels. I had bought a score of nightlights to set the scene in my cabin.

Jackie was at the bar, sipping iced water. I took the nearest stool.

'Thought I'd better alert you - Manus is running late. He was still in the shower when I left.'

Jackie knew my brother's habits. We'd have an hour to ourselves before my brother appeared. He smiled and I knew that I hadn't misread the signals. This is it, I thought, tonight's the night.

We were settling down in a quiet nook when a familiar figure charged through the door. I'd never seen my brother so punctual - or so agitated. He blundered across the room.

'You have to talk some sense into Kara. She's walking herself into a heap of trouble.'

***

We reached the pier in time to see my sister slither down the ladder into my father's punt. The motorboat danced on a skittish tide.

'Where the hell does she think she's doing?' I asked.

'They're going ahead with the cull tonight, before the guards get word. There's a rake of boats heading for the Inish.'

'And Kara thinks she can stop them?'

We listened to her attempts to start the engine. It clanked and died with a whine.

'Does she know how to handle a boat?' Jackie asked.

Manus shook his head. 'She'll never get it going.'

I knew better. Kara was stubborn enough to persist though she hadn't a clue about setting a course. 'We can't let her head out there on her own. She'll be carried out to sea,' I said.

My brother was swaying on his feet. Just standing on the pier was enough to make him dizzy.

'I'm not going out in no boat.'

As he limped away the motor caught and turned.

I shimmied down the ladder. The boat shifted with the weight of someone landing behind me.

'You're not going to stop me,' Kara shouted.

'I'm just on for the spin,' Jackie said.

***

The Inish was a black hump against the darkness; a cliff face that rose sheer out of the sea. Taking the punt round to the beach on the seaward side, we saw that the island was speckled with moving circles of light. Here and there burning torches gave added light to the night's work. Kara whimpered at the sounds that carried over the water. As we eased into the shallows she was up and over the side.

Two lads stood sentry on the shore. When they saw my sister running, they came striding across the strand with outflung arms. This was men's work - not for the eyes of women. There was a scuffle and a scream as someone went down. I dropped anchor and leapt over the side, but Jackie outpaced me, splashing through the last few feet of water.

One of the lads was writhing on the ground. The other hung onto Kara. Just in time, he saw the knee aiming for his groin. He took a side step, loosening his hold and she was off. His friend was still clutching the front of his trousers.

'Sorry, she's not herself,' I explained.

'She's loop-the-loop, all right.'

Somewhat appeased, the lads backed down. It was almost over anyhow - time to retrieve the six-pack they'd hidden in the rocks. Jackie took my arm and we went to find Kara.

Ahead we could make out figures moving in a line. Some held torches, while others executed the business. They worked silently, never looking back, focused on what was caught in the beam of their lights. Night draped a shroud on what they left in their wake. I tried to close my senses against the smell of fresh blood, the *thunk* of club against bone, the moans of injured seals. Jackie had gone still, and I felt the need to explain these desperate measures. He cut me off, pointing in the direction of raised voices. My sister was at the centre of a gathering crowd, shouting abuse. Someone was trying to placate her. 'These things have to be done, dear.' The voice was calm, reasoning.

Kara thumped the speaker square in the chest, and he stumbled, caught off guard by the force of the blow. She continued to lash out when I pulled her back.

'For God's sake, Kara. Cop yourself on!'

'Ah, you wouldn't expect a young one to understand.'

The men turned their backs, walking away. They were anxious to get out of this place, back to their boats, back to port. There was a muttered complaint about unwed mothers, living off the state. The speaker dropped his guttering brand and turned back to direct a parting shot. 'Easy for them that don't have to bust their balls just to scrape a few bob. Do you not think we'd all sooner be snug in our bunks?'

Shadows fell in around us as the lights retreated across the island. Jackie picked up the smouldering torch, blowing on it until it rekindled. We began to make our way back to the beach. In the quiet we heard a whimper. Kara grabbed the torch and a gust of air flamed through it, throwing light on a seal pup. It was alive. Barely.

She dropped to her knees, reaching out as if to pet the creature; recoiled as it shuddered. The pup was beyond help. She looked up into our faces and we knew what needed to be done. Nobody moved.

The seal's cries went through me. 'It'll be dead soon anyway. Come on away to hell out of here.'

I had walked a few yards when I heard a *thump*.

The whimpers stopped abruptly. Turning, I saw Kara struggle to her feet, a rock in her hand. Her legs began to give way. We rushed to support her and I saw that her fingers were wrapped around the bloodied stone. I tried to loosen it from her grasp. 'You can throw it away now.' She pulled her hand away, shoving it into the pocket of her jacket.

'Shock,' Jackie whispered. 'Let it be for now.'

On the way ashore, she sat seething in a corner of the boat.

***

Back at the pier I accepted Jackie's offer of a lift home. No amount of tea lights would restore this night. Kara jumped into the front seat, still wordless. Her mood settled over us, forbidding conversation until we reached the house. I thanked Jackie for his support.
'No bother,' he said, before I had a chance to ask him in for tea. 'See you around.'

The brush-off. I sauntered up the path as if it didn't matter. So much for seduction. The soles of my shoes were sucking off the cement, sticky with blood.

***

When I came down for breakfast, my mother was eyeing the object in the middle of the kitchen table. Set on a sheet of newspaper, it looked worse in daylight, covered with gore and matted fur. Kara spooned egg into Daniel's mouth.

'How could you feed the baby with that thing sitting there?' I braced myself to lift the edges of the newspaper.

'Don't you dare touch it,' Kara said.

My mother stepped in. 'You're upset. This thing will only keep it in your head. Throw it away, love.'

'Do you think I'd forget? It's not for me. It's for the rest of you. So the next time you're mouthing off about killing defenceless animals, at least you'll know what you're talking about.'

I turned to my father. 'Tell her she's being an asshole.'

Stenk laid down his newspaper and considered the rock.

'The truth is neither good nor bad - it is merely the truth.'

Solomon had spoken. The rock would stay, though my mother insisted on washing it. She scrubbed until her fingers were raw, but she couldn't rinse the stains away – the blood had seeped into the limestone surface.

***

Gaia arrived that evening. There was a crowd on the pier to watch her come in. I saw my father's covetous expression as we stood admiring the vessel, a four-mast schooner, perfectly restored.

'It was a tall ship that took French Willie off to fish the Newfoundland Banks. Great-great-granda did his share of sealing when the fishing failed out there.'

'Don't let Kara hear you saying that.'

'They were hard times, Val. People did what they had to do.'

'These are hard times. Fish is scarce enough without bloody seals taking the bite out of the fishermen's mouths. Everyone knows they're breeding out of control.'

'Seals won't be the problem once the salmon fishing ban comes in.'

'They can't do that.'

'But they will, *girseach*, you may depend on it.'

The crew of the ship stepped onto the pier and Radio Annie was there to meet them. We watched her aim the microphone. Eyebrows were raised when the skipper stepped forward, a woman leathered by time and sea. She responded with the energy of someone half her age, outraged at having arrived too late.

'We'll compile a report,' she said, 'but statistics have little emotional impact - not without an eyewitness account.' Annie glanced across at us, and I knew what she was thinking.

***

Kara took the visitors into the living room. They stayed a long time. My mother brought them tea, returning to the kitchen in a steer.

'They're making a study of seal colonies. Eighteen months round the British Isles. They want to take Kara away with them. She's that mad about this whole thing, I wouldn't put it past her.'

She waited anxiously until the visitors had left; pouncing on my sister when she'd closed the door behind them.

'Well? Are you going away with them?'

Kara looked at our mother as if she was cracked. Her soft nature had propelled her into action - but she was no fighter. She wouldn't stray far from her comfort zone.

The old boy grunted. 'They asked the wrong sister. Val would have jumped at the chance.'

'You forget I'm on the wrong side,' I said.

'What of it? If I was your age, I'd adopt any philosophy for the chance to sail a ship like that.'

'They said it's going to happen again if I don't speak out.' Kara lifted the stone and stared hard at it. 'People have to be told. It's the only way to stop it.'

***

Annie set up the interview with Seaboard radio, though she warned it might be tough. Donal, her boss, was confrontational. When they returned from the studio we could see the way it had gone. My mother prised the story out of Kara.

'He asked if I knew how many tons of fish it took to support a colony. Then he started quoting figures. I don't know stuff like that. Every time I spoke he corrected me. I felt so stupid.'

Stenk was philosophical. 'You didn't know your facts, love. Let it be a lesson.'

When we listened to the interview on the news that night, his temperate mood vanished. 'Self-righteous little pup. Did you hear him badgering her? She never got a chance to say her piece.'

He slapped the phone book on the table, flicking through until he found a number. When he came off the phone he had the look of a warrior. He had spoken to a woman in the Marine Department. 'She's sending us the latest research.'

Kara cast a huffy look at him. 'What's the point? I've blown it now.'

'Ach, who listens to Seaboard Radio? We'll get onto the big boys.'

As spokesman for the Fisherman's League, my father had friends in the media. A television crew arrived to film what they called 'the carnage on the Inish'. They spoke to Kara briefly, but declined an interview. The pictures were enough.

Kara seemed relieved. It was a surprise to see her bent over the notes the marine biologist had sent. The more she studied them, the more frustrated she became. 'It's useless. I can't hack this techno jargon.'

My father suggested a course in the Regional. Sixty miles wasn't that far away - she could get a flat. My mother jumped in with an offer to mind the baby. At this point Kara ran upstairs to our bedroom. The old boy rolled his eyes.

'There's gratitude. You offer her a chance and she

couldn't be arsed.'

***

It was a weekend for unexpected visitors. A stranger sat at the kitchen table. Suited, clean-shaven, his face was two-toned, deeply tanned from brow to cheekbones and unnaturally pale beneath.

Manus was not impressed. 'What'll we call you now, Jackie the Beardless?'

Admiring the cut of Jackie's suit, I thought of the red silk camisole. I was dressed in my oldest jeans, my father's baggy jumper, and sludge-grey underwear from my mother's boil wash.

'Well,' he said, 'what's the verdict? Am I clean-cut enough to take you out to dinner?'

'You'll do.' If he had revealed the features of a deep-sea gurnard, I'd have thought the same. I was seeing past the two-toned face, beyond skin, bone and gristle.

I rushed for the bedroom to throw on my best dress. Kara was on the bed, trying to read her notes while Daniel slammed his little fist on the pages. Instead of putting him down, she sat there, tears dripping onto the paper. I figured it out then, the way it had probably hit her earlier. The marine biology course was made for her, a chance to live away from home, her best chance to break free of my mother's protective web. But she'd have to leave Daniel, and she'd never do that.

***

Over dinner, Jackie unfolded his plans. 'I have the offer of a contract in the States when we finish in Malaysia. It's a good gig, consultancy work. But I've a mind to settle home and start up a wee business. You only have to say the word.'

If Jackie was expecting an ecstatic response, he showed no surprise at my hesitation.

'Maybe I spoke too soon. A proposal on a first date is a bit premature. I like to be straight about things.' He took a sip from his mineral water. 'I won't pretend I've lead a sheltered life. But a well-travelled man makes a good husband - and a good father.'

It was the last bit that did it, the word that suggested my part in all this. He'd been everywhere, done everything. What had I done? Nothing. No way was I ready for maternity.

'Actually, I have plans of my own. *Gaia* is short a crewman - and I'm an experienced hand.'

As soon as the words were out of my mouth, I knew it was what I wanted.

***

It was gone four by the time I tiptoed into our bedroom. My sister was still at the books, a sleeping Daniel in the crook of her arm. His head was almost touching the stone where she'd set it on the bedside table. She squeezed her eyes shut.

'I can't do this on my own. Do you think they

have part-time courses in the Regional?'

'It would be a long, slow haul that way."

'I'll do it, if it takes ten years. I want to be able to talk the way you do. Like you know you're right.'

'Maybe I am right.'

'No. I don't want Daniel growing up in a world where life means nothing.'

'It's not as if it was human life.'

'They're gunning down street kids in Brazil for stealing food. Stealing *food*, Val.'

'You know that's not the same.'

For answer she took my hand and guided it to the stone, pressing my fingers against the killing edge. I knew then, blood moon or no blood moon, we would never agree. But I recognised that steely core, the awkward streak that would lead us down any twisting path – bar the easy road.

Kara's nose was buried in the book again. I lifted the baby from her arms, gently, so as not to disturb either of them, and laid him to rest in his cot.

Home Cooking

Clarrie Pringle

'He who believes in me and dies shall live forever and he who lives and believes in me shall never die.'

Maggie sighed contentedly. She just loved it when they used these words at the funerals. It was confirmation for her. The first time she had heard them, or noticed, really, was at her husband's funeral. She had taken great comfort from them; they had lifted a heavy burden from her shoulders.

The words of Jesus to Lazarus' sisters had given her the courage to continue. It was a relief – she had never looked on death in quite that way before John's tragic end. It seemed like only yesterday, though it was fifteen years ago now. Married at nineteen, widowed at thirty-four, she was thankful they had not had children, and grateful that she had had the foresight to take out life insurance on John a year before his death. Whatever had possessed her? She giggled inwardly, remembering.

Surprising how simple it had been, fill in the

form, tell the truth, sign it, and Bob's your uncle. Getting the money to pay for the coverage had taken a bit longer, gathering a wee bit here, a punt there, but she had made it. The term 'rude good health' had certainly applied to him. Yes, she would always be grateful to him for leaving her so comfortably off.

Funerals were certainly times for remembering. She always attended alone. Maggie loved them, found them particularly satisfying. It was peculiar, really, sometimes she expected the widow and family to come up and shake her hand, and had to remind herself that she was a stranger to the mourners. Of course, Maggie was never a stranger to the deceased. She sometimes thought it would be nice to have an occasional acknowledgement of her efforts at the funeral.

As the music started, Maggie examined the grieving widow minutely from her vantage point in the gallery. Young enough, about forty, she reckoned, tired face, drooping, just like her shoulders. Psyching herself up, Maggie sent her mental message to the widow: 'You'll be fine, fine, you'll have a grand life now, don't worry.' She repeated it a few times to make sure it got through and was pleased to notice a little lightening around the eyes and a slight straightening of the shoulders. She knew her message had been received and the widow had had a brief glimpse of a possibly shiny future. Good. Maggie was satisfied.

Widows definitely needed moral support. Maggie knew from experience that guilt played a major part in the mourning process. Guilt, the feeling of a burden being lifted, the titillation of freedom, the realization of self. Yes, there was the discovery of a person, a real one, not someone's housekeeper, cleaner or cook.

This death was probably a shock to the wife, knocked her sideways for a while. *Whereas I was well prepared for John, so it didn't hit me too hard.* Maggie sighed contentedly as she ambled away from the church, send-off over.

It hadn't taken her too long to get organized after John died, her heart swelling with excitement till she thought it would burst. Three months of busy mourning had resulted in the opening of her little cafe, simply called Maggie's Place. She had the respect and admiration of extended family and friends for her great courage in 'pulling herself together'. She often thought the word, 'herself', was just right.

Her wholesome cooking was certainly appreciated and the word soon spread far and wide. Maggie was well established in no time, with a regular clientele from the offices and factories in the neighbourhood. She tried not to feel too smug all these years later, relishing her foresight. She had long reckoned her only talent had been for cooking and homemaking – at least John had told her so often enough.

Maggie had married a few months after finishing school, leaving her parents' home to set up a new one with her brand-new husband. For a while it felt like she was playing house, but Maggie really knew she had made a lovely home for John and herself – even turning the wilderness of the big back garden into an oasis of scented greenery, including a vegetable patch. Everyone complimented her on her efforts in those early years.

***

She was Queen of her Castle then, and sometimes she was a little nostalgic for those days. John, ten years her senior, had said they would wait a few years before starting a family until he was well established, and she was a bit older. It suited Maggie, particularly as John, an accountant, worked so hard keeping all his clients' money right.

It was a responsible position and he really burned the midnight oil, working late, even the occasional weekend, as time went by. He sometimes had to go away overnight midweek as well, but Maggie never complained of loneliness. It gave her the time to work hard in the garden. She usually had a nice casserole or pie waiting for John on his return home, no matter how late it was. Everything healthy and good, vegetables and fresh herbs grown by her own hand long before 'organic' became the in thing for all the weedy wimps, and always a homemade pie for afters, smothered in cream. John had a great appetite in those days, too. It was only in later years that she learned *why* he needed to keep up his strength. She smiled now, thinking on it.

He used to tell her she was 'the perfect little

wife', not like some of those hard hussies of career women he came across at work. He sometimes ranted about the 'liberation' of women who were bringing problems into the workforce when they should know their place was in the home. John rarely spoke to her about his work or individuals in his office. He would say he wanted to keep his two worlds separate. Anyway, he knew she wouldn't understand.

Oh yes, for those first five or six years life had been wonderful for Maggie, even though she had gradually lost contact with her school friends, all of whom had careers then. The odd time she was feeling a bit down she would remind herself of the good things she had – the house, big garden, no stress. Her unfortunate unmarried friends must have envied her, though she admitted privately they hid it well.

She had thought at one time she might get a little job for herself, just to pass the time. John was totally against it, though – no wife of his would have to work. The garden really became her haven then. Maggie perfected her cooking skills, always experimenting and later growing her own vegetables and herbs – even tomatoes in the tiny glasshouse John had given her one Christmas. How useful now for her thriving business. She was a great believer in putting all her talents to good use.

Maggie was considering retiring from the restaurant, regretful she had no one to pass on her skills to, though she knew no one would ever continue her very specialized work. Thirty years in all, if you counted it from the time she married – fifteen in training, fifteen in action. And still young enough now at forty-nine for new career options. Was it time to finally concentrate on her own pleasure?

When Maggie first discovered all those years ago that her wonderful John was unfaithful to her, she had been devastated. She needed time to build up her courage to mention it to him. She watched and waited until her suspicions were confirmed. People had been hinting for a long time, of course, but she hadn't understood.

Maggie had been oblivious until she found the bracelet in the car. Simple links, plain, but very gold and classy – no one she knew wore anything like this. Shock silenced her, and it took some courage for her to finally accept the truth. Everything fell in to place then. The hints of friends, the overtime, nights away - it all fit.

She decided not to confront him at all, to let things continue as normal. He was a great liar. She really had to admire him for it. When the anonymous letter from the young one in the office finally arrived, Maggie was grateful. Confirmation. Imagine, he'd had so many, getting younger all the time. The career women he complained about to her didn't seem to bother him at all when he was on the hunt. Maggie kept her silence, though she was alert now and watchful.

Their life didn't change. She needed time to think, to weigh up the pros and cons. She would do nothing hasty. No, she would learn from him. Plan. There was no point in leaving, sure where would she go? She loved her house and garden. So Maggie plotted, even as she gardened. Her herbs flourished, particularly the digitalis. Her brain was set in motion, put to use at last. The cooking improved, got more adventurous.

John loved sampling the new recipes, playing a game of trying to identify the herbs and spices. He was always missing out on her 'special secret', teasing her affectionately. The patronizing shit. Though, poor John, his stomach wasn't what it used to be, she sometimes mentioned to friends. Maggie often had to experiment with herbal remedies for him, sometimes using the algae of the wild Atlantic to help the flavours. The restorative powers of the fruits of the ocean were long known locally. She was really an excellent wife – everyone said so, remarking how she 'doted on him'. She got great satisfaction from taking care of him, and she let it be known it did her heart good. Her patience eventually paid off as she knew it would, her wonderful herbs having their long-desired effect.

She sighed contentedly now as she remembered the last few minutes of his life. He had come clean in the end, confessing, holding her hand in his. He told her he was sorry, that he had loved only her, the others meant nothing. He said that who and how many were irrelevant, that he always came home to her. The confession helped Maggie, too. She gave him her full forgiveness. Oh no, she wouldn't want anyone to end their life with a guilty conscience. She liked to think he went straight to heaven – well, with maybe a little detour on the way.

At John's funeral she speculated as she studied the mourners covertly: Who amongst those from the office had been kind enough to give her the tip-off and confirm her mission? Was it the pretty little receptionist with the giggle that so irritated John? Or the one John had named "Sourpuss", who took care of the accounts and quibbled over every penny of his expense claims? Maggie would probably never know, but she wasn't too pushed either. She was just grateful to her unknown benefactor, who had confirmed her choice of a new career. The letter had come after her own suspicions, but the independent confirmation kept her from wavering.

*****

When she opened the restaurant Maggie made a financial success of it. Eventually she employed a couple of reliable women to help, usually mothers who were having a hard time making ends meet. Her staff loved her. She used all the skills acquired during her marriage, creating a restaurant with a reputation for good, simple food and a homely ambience. The customers responded warmly to her smiling good humour and obvious enjoyment of her work.

As her regular clientele built up, she supposed it

was only natural that men would make a few passes. After all, she wasn't bad looking, kept herself nice, and was friendly to everyone. It wasn't her problem that some of the male customers mistook her friendly nature for something else. But it did set her thinking. They were usually middle-aged, professional men, probably testosterone-threatened, going through male menopausal crisis or whatever. A bit like her John, really, except his mid-life crisis started extra early.

To a certain extent, Maggie encouraged them. She sat talking with them, gave them a warm smile of welcome when they'd come in. She was only doing her research, seeking to ascertain whether they'd cheated on their wives before, or if they were all talk and no action. She didn't rush into anything, had to be sure. When she was certain, well, she knew what she had to do – wasn't it her mission in life? She was a zealous missionary.

Now there were a few more widows who owed their freedom to Maggie. Pity she couldn't let them know. Might be nice to compare notes.

As she left the church, blessing herself with the holy water, anonymous amongst the gathering of mourners, she counted up how many women she had helped over the years. She reckoned there were nine in all.

She was delighted that she was religious; it was such a comfort. She knew her work would be more difficult if she didn't believe in the words of Jesus. Would she have started out on her mission otherwise?

Maggie really didn't know. Religion here in Ireland was always a great source of inspiration to her. It gave her a sense of security to know she would always be welcome in God's house. How silly she had been when she was young to resent the presence of the Very Important People lining the front rows of the church, receiving Holy Communion before anyone else, along with the special smile of acknowledgment from the parish priest. Proved what they said: God loves sinners, even those who stole from the poor, treated people like slaves, sexually satisfied themselves with other people's children – as she knew from personal experience. It was only recently in her maturity she found God's love so comforting.

Maggie knew she could have helped a lot more women with her garden produce over the years, but she had to be careful. She wouldn't want the reputation of the restaurant to be affected – male regulars suddenly disappearing after brief illnesses? No, no, she had to be very selective. It was more satisfying to decide who was the most deserving. She had actually had a fling with a few of the customers in the early years, too, but only for research purposes. It helped her decision-making and it had been fun – well, mostly. But this funeral may be the last act of her charitable deed. She'd miss that aspect of her work. What would be the appropriate business term? Liquidating her assets? She smiled smugly. Yes, she had done good for the sisterhood over the years. Still, time to move on.

Incredibly, she had actually fallen for the latest subject of her research. Really, she supposed, she had allowed herself to grow fond of him when she discovered he wasn't married, though he did have that married air about him. He was actually a widower, and still grieving for his wife when she met him – he was missing his home comforts. That had touched her.

He seemed genuine enough, so when he suggested they marry after four months of his paying for her home cooking and company, she considered it for a while. No hasty decisions. He left it entirely up to her whether she continued to work in the restaurant or not. He told her he wouldn't want to change her, said he loved her as she was. That was very gratifying, really. She could do whatever pleased her, he would never stand in her way – or so he said. She agreed.

Maggie didn't quite believe him, but decided she'd give him the benefit of the doubt. She might possibly feel something for him too, which could be a plus. At the same time, she doubted it would last, living under the same roof. But either way she looked forward to the challenge.

Another career option. She knew she wouldn't be stuck if it didn't work out.

She would always have her garden.

Stargazing

Charlie Garratt

A frown clouded the pretty face of Gráinne Gallagher, though she managed to maintain the pleasant telephone voice she always used for library customers, regardless of how troublesome they might be.

'Yes Mr O'Donnell, your books are still here, one on Saturn and one on the Crab Nebula. They've been waiting under the counter for a week. When will you be in to collect them?'

The young woman's brow furrowed even further.

'I'm sorry to hear you've not been well but it's very unusual, you know.' Gráinne dropped the frown, and plunged her ladle into the milk of human kindness. 'I suppose I could drop them off on my way home, Mr O'Donnell. Would eight o'clock be all right?'

***

There was no answer from the doorbell at Seamie O'Donnell's house, so Gráinne peered through the letterbox, then called his name a couple of times. If she'd been one for cursing this would have been the occasion to do it. She'd puffed the detour on her bicycle, fighting the Donegal landscape all the way, and now it seemed the amateur astronomer had forgotten their arrangement.

The librarian considered, against her better judgement, leaving the tomes on the back step. Gráinne had spent the last month rereading the entire series of Sherlock Holmes stories, her current passion, and she had the final collection of his cases in her basket. She'd wrapped the book in a plastic bag, alongside the astronomy books, to protect all of them against any potential rain. The ones she'd brought to Seamie were expensive and she knew there'd be the devil to pay if they were damaged. Gráinne took the bag containing the reference books and offered a prayer to the saints that her boss wouldn't find out what she'd done.

She passed down the path between the garage and the house, then saw a chink of light shining through a gap between the panelling on a large shed. As Gráinne crossed the lawn towards the building, she tripped on a hosepipe that lay in the grass, and yelped as she cracked her knee on the ground.

'Who's there?'

'It's only me, Mr O'Donnell, Gráinne Gallagher from the library.'

Dusting herself off, she found her way to the door and stepped inside. The interior was as far from a simple garden shed as Gráinne could imagine. In the centre stood an enormous telescope, dominating the available space, and the walls were covered with charts and photographs of the night sky. Seated in a leather armchair was a man in his seventies, balding and wearing a Donegal tweed suit with the waistcoat unbuttoned.

'Are you all right Miss Gallagher? Not hurt yourself I hope? It can be a bit treacherous out there.' He pointed upwards. 'I spend a little more time looking into the heavens than at my own garden I'm afraid.'

Gráinne assured the astronomer that she was fine, though feeling a little foolish, and handed him the books.

'You will take care and return them on time, won't you?'

With the elderly man's assurances tucked away, Gráinne freewheeled her bike down to the main road, glowing with the warmth of doing her good deed for the day and looking forward to a night with her favourite detective.

*****

It was the usual crowd of last-minute stragglers in the library as the clock ticked towards closing time. Mr Byrne, saving on his electricity bill and the price of a daily newspaper, was always one of the last to leave and Gráinne wondered, not for the first time, if Mrs Breslin struggled to make all decisions or just those involving library books. She'd been in three times this week as usual, and still hadn't arrived at what she was taking home for her weekend's reading.

With everyone out of the door at last, Gráinne was finally turning the key when the indecisive Mrs Breslin returned. The librarian's heart sank.

'Oh, I'm so sorry, Miss Gallagher, I forgot to tell you about Mr O'Donnell. You knew him, didn't you?'

'Only really as a borrower, Mrs Breslin. 'Has something happened to him?'

'He passed away, I'm afraid. Didn't turn up for lunch with a friend so they came round and found him in that shed of his. The family have asked for the wake to be private but the funeral is tomorrow at twelve.'

***

There was only a small group at the graveside, and Gráinne presumed this was what happened when one grows older, with fewer and fewer friends to mourn your passing. Father Boyle spoke nicely and Gráinne was more than pleased when he asked if she'd join them at Seamie's house for a sandwich and a little refreshment. She needed to retrieve the books she'd left and hadn't quite worked out how she could do so without seeming callous.

Gráinne offered her condolences to the relatives and chatted to some of her library regulars for a while. One of them was a scatty young man about her own age, more interested in securing a date than paying his respects to the family of the deceased Mr O'Donnell. After ten minutes warding off his advances, she escaped with her cigarettes and her thoughts into the garden.

Seamie O'Donnell, she'd been informed by a niece, had died in his armchair and it was assumed he'd been getting ready for his night's stargazing when he'd suffered a heart attack or stroke. The final results of the autopsy hadn't yet been released but it was known he'd had high blood pressure, so one of these was the most likely cause of his demise. Gráinne had remarked to the niece that she'd been quite shocked by the uncle's death because he'd looked so well the last time she'd seen him.

It occurred to Gráinne that her library's books might still be in the makeshift observatory, so she wandered over to take a look. Before going in she drew a final few drags, hoping to appear nonchalant as she circled the outside to ensure no one was watching. On the side of the shed where she'd tripped a few evenings earlier, she was surprised to see the errant hose was no longer lying there. Thinking she may have kicked it away when it caught her foot, she searched the surrounding area but it was nowhere to be found. Despite herself, she wondered what Holmes would have made of its disappearance. For a moment or two she mused about how Watson might have written it up as "The Case of the Missing Pipe", and Gráinne chuckled at her silliness.

The shed door wasn't locked and everything

appeared to be much the way it had been when she was last there, with the obvious exception of the presence of Mr O'Donnell, and the pieces of a broken plate that lay at the side of his chair where it must have fallen when he took his last breath. *At least,* Gráinne thought, *he managed to finish his supper before he went.* Then she saw the roof hatch above the telescope was also closed and recalled it had been wide open on the night she visited. She wondered if the gardaí would have bothered to close it. She felt certain Holmes would have noted all of these things from his cursory inspection of the room and then come to the conclusion that something wasn't quite right.

***

Maura Fitzpatrick's garden was a picture, with rose bushes of every habit and colour and containers chock full of busy Lizzies, fuchsia and begonia.

That scent is divine, how does she find the time? thought Gráinne when she strolled up the path, pausing to admire through the open garage door the shine on Maura's prize possession, a 1955 Morris Minor.–A hoe, rake and myriad garden tools hung ready for action along one wall.

Her friend's house was next door to the unfortunate Seamie O'Donnell's home and Gráinne could see the side of his shed through the hedge that divided the two properties. Maura took a few moments to answer her doorbell, apologising for the delay and for the flour that dusted her apron and hands.

'I've been up to my ears in baking, Gráinne, come through to the kitchen. I assume you're here about the coffee morning?'

'Aye, though it's not just a coffee morning, more of an open day at the library. Trying to get new people interested, not that it works very often. Do you think you could let us have a few cakes? The ones you put into last month's competition at the festival were tremendous. First prize, I seem to remember.'

Maura blushed and put on the kettle. Gráinne looked around the kitchen.

'Very tidy worker you are Maura. Not a speck of flour anywhere.'

'Oh … er … I'd just tidied up when you rang at the door. Hadn't quite got cleaned myself. Terrible about Seamie, wasn't it? I often saw him from the window going into his shed. I'd drop him round the odd vanilla slice from time to time, you know, and he did love them. So sad.'

***

With Maura's donation of a few plates of fancy cakes in her bag, Gráinne said her goodbyes and wandered round to take another look in the observatory. She was trying to make sense of the nagging thoughts that had entered her head whilst sipping her tea. She knew her Sherlock Holmes addiction was making her fanciful but she couldn't get the missing hosepipe and the closed shed roof out of her thoughts.

The crumbs still lay on the floor and Gráinne lifted one to sniff. There was little doubt that Seamie had been enjoying one of Maura's vanilla slices the night he died. The librarian thought it strange she hadn't mentioned taking him one so close to his last breath.

She decided to go through the shed one more time in search of the missing books but had no luck until she spied a small cupboard at head height on the wall closest to Maura's house. Inside, neatly stacked, were the two volumes and Gráinne cursed that she'd missed them the first time. On top of them was a pair of binoculars. As she was closing the door she noticed the cupboard was hinged at the back and she could swing it away from the wall. There was a hole cut in the woodwork, just about big enough to poke the binoculars through, and to the librarian's surprise she could see straight in to Maura's kitchen.

***

Gráinne wouldn't normally buy a sandwich at lunchtime, preferring to save cash and calories by taking in fruit or pasta from home but she'd slept badly, and today was covering for a sick colleague in the library in the neighbouring town. Dreams of stolen books, dead astronomers, plucky female detectives and vanilla slices had disturbed her night. As a result, she'd woken late and barely had time to gobble her granola before cycling off for the bus. She reasoned that her midday walk to the shops would partly compensate for the negative effects of the carbohydrates and fat she was about to buy. Anyway, why shouldn't she treat herself once in a while?

The Shamrock Slice was a bakery at the far end of The Diamond, and a den of temptation Gráinne would usually avoid. She had a vague hope she might convince the owner to make a contribution to the library open day, so she'd decided to kill two birds with one stone and splash out on her lunch at the same time. The window was a delight, a veritable embroidery of chocolate, meringue, sponge, cream and icing. Inside, the combination of sweetness and baking bread sent Gráinne reeling and reminded her why she didn't go in more often. A young woman in a blue starched dress and white cap asked if she could help.

'I'll have a prawn salad sandwich, on wholemeal, please. Oh, and one of those lovely pink iced buns from the window. Could you pop the cake in a box for me, it's a present for a friend. I think she might be a customer of yours - Mrs Maura Fitzpatrick?'

***

This time Maura answered her door quickly.

'Oh, Gráinne, it's nice to see you again so soon. To what do I owe the pleasure?'

'I've brought you something. In fact I've brought one for both of us. Is the kettle on? She placed a white cardboard box on the kitchen table. 'Here, put these on a plate.'

Maura opened the lid and looked quizzical.

'Why have you brought me two of my own cakes back? Is there something wrong with them?'

'Nothing at all, Maura, they're perfect. Just like the ones you won the baking competition with. Only trouble is they're not yours, are they? One is. Well I mean it's the one you gave me, but you didn't actually bake it did you? The other is from that cake shop, the Shamrock Slice. Uncannily similar, don't you think?'

'Such ungrateful insinuations. I've never been so insulted in my whole life.'

'Come, come, Maura, you must have been. Isn't this what Seamie discovered then threatened to expose you? I think he'd secretly been watching you in your kitchen through his binoculars, for reasons I shudder to imagine, and saw you putting the shop-bought cakes on plates for the competition. When he confronted you there was no option other than getting rid of him, was there?'

Maura slumped into a chair. 'I never meant for it to go so far. At first he just wanted the occasional cupcake when he was stargazing, then he stepped up to vanilla slices. It was costing me a fortune. Finally, one evening he made … suggestions. Explained he'd seen me wandering round the kitchen in the mornings in my housecoat and that he wanted more than cakes. Well, I couldn't, could I?'

'If my hero Mr Holmes had been on the case he'd

have easily figured out you took Seamie one more vanilla slice, spiked with sleeping pills this time. He'd have known you waited until the astronomer nodded off before running the hosepipe from your car exhaust into the shed, knocking the prop from the roof opening with your rake, then waited for the fumes to do their work. Your only mistake was to leave the hose outside until after the funeral. I assume you imagined no one would give it a second thought.'

'Silly of me. Instead of pulling it back to my side I panicked and cut it off at the fence. It was only later I realised someone might guess, so then I ran round and collected it.'

They stared at each other in silence for what seemed an age. Eventually, Maura cracked.

'So what are you going to do?'

'There was only one thing I could do when I worked it out – with Sherlock's help of course. I called the gardaí. They'll be round shortly.'

Maura poured two fresh cups of tea and smiled. 'Shall we have one of those buns you brought while we're waiting?'

The Foyle
Darren Gallagher

'What do you think we'll catch today, Dad?' Brian looked upriver to where they had left the town behind. The current was slow, and his father was rowing them downstream to their quiet spot, where they knew the fish were plentiful. It was midsummer, even though dull grey clouds suggested otherwise.

'I'm not sure, son. I guess we'll just have to wait and see.' Conor smiled. He enjoyed these days he spent fishing with his son. This time next year Brian would be a teenager, and would want to do things other than go fishing with his old man.

Conor stopped rowing and let the boat glide to a stop in the middle of the Foyle, the largest river in Donegal. A few miles upstream the rivers Finn and Mourne came together to birth it. Today it was unusually calm, but Conor didn't mind. It meant he wouldn't have to keep rowing the boat away from the banks, or row an extra mile or two back home again. Brian lifted his fishing rod as his father cradled the oars on the side of the boat. They had set up the rods before leaving. He cast upstream and the *plop* echoed as his father grabbed his rod and sat next to him.

'Someone's a little eager today?' He smiled.

'I want to get the first catch. You get it all the time.' Brian reeled in the line slowly.

His father laughed. 'Well, whoever lands the first one, the other has to gut it. Deal?'

'Get your knife ready then.' Brian laughed with him.

Conor cast his line in the opposite direction, but nothing was biting today. They had been here over an hour and still nothing nibbled.

'What do you think, Brian? Should we call it a day?'

'Not yet. Let's at least catch something first.'

'Right, okay.'

Something splashed in the water behind them. Conor looked over his shoulder and saw ripples. 'Well at least we know there are fish here.'

Brian reeled in his line quicker this time and cast it straight out. Something broke the surface of the water not far from where he had cast, and an arrow of ripples came toward them. They couldn't see what was making it.

'Bring it in a little faster,' Conor said, encouraging and focused.

His own rod jerked in his hands and almost went into the river, catching him completely unaware. Conor was fast enough to catch it, but whatever was on his line was stronger than he'd expected. He reeled in the line a little and pulled the rod back into the air, then lowered it before reeling again.

'Oh, it's a big one son,' he said, struggling.

Brian wasn't watching his father however; he was more interested in the ripples appearing in the water around them. He counted seven different sets, but he couldn't see what was making them. Normally the fish jumped out of the water, splashing and creating circular patterns. Sometimes they would open their mouths at the surface, creating smaller circles, but these were unusual, very strange.

'Get the net ready, son; I think I nearly have him. Looks like you'll be the one doing the gutting.' He attempted a smile but the fish was making him use all his strength, and his face crumpled with the effort.

Brian lifted the net and kept it near the edge of the boat. Just then, another arrowhead-shaped ripple appeared directly beside them and Brian stared into the water.

He saw what had made it, but it didn't make sense. The fish resembled a giant koi, but it had rows of spikes sticking out all over its body. It was metallic grey with flashes of red and orange where the spikes protruded from the skin. Brian didn't like the look of it.

'Dad ... I don't think you should pull that in.'

'Don't be getting jealous now,' Conor said. He hadn't seen what was beside their boat.

'I'm serious, Dad. There's something wrong with

these fish.'

'Nonsense, Brian. What could be wrong with them?' Conor continued to reel it in; it was nearly at the boat now.

More ripples circled the boat. 'Dad, seriously. I don't like this.' He started to shift uncomfortably, and the boat swayed.

'It's fine son, just relax. They can't do you any harm.'

Conor pulled the rod back once more, and a few feet from the boat the fish splashed furiously in an attempt to get free. For the first time Conor saw what was making his son uneasy. In the thirty years he had been fishing, he'd never seen anything like what was now on his line.

It was about three-foot long, and from the way it thrashed back and forth, Conor knew this fish had more strength than it was letting on.

'What it is, Dad?' Brian saw the look on his father's face.

'I'm not sure, son.'

'There are more swimming around the boat.'

Conor still looked confused. 'Get the knife.'

Brian dived into the bag with their provisions. Just as he pulled back the zip something slammed into the boat. He looked at his father, frightened. Then it happened again.

'Hurry, Brian.'

He reached into the bag, grabbed the knife and looked to his father for direction.

'Cut the line.'

Brian scrambled over and put the blade to the taut line, but it went slack before he had a chance to cut it. The fish leaped out of the water and stared directly at them before it fell back into the river.

'Cut it!' Conor urged again.

The fish's head appeared at the top of the water just as Brian was about to cut the line. It puffed out its cheeks and spikes shot toward them. Conor jumped backwards and pulled Brian with him. One of the spikes pierced the rod; another lodged in Conor's finger. A third spike was sticking out of Brian's face where his jawbone met his ear. His face had already started to swell.

'Brian!' Conor dropped the fishing rod and grabbed hold of his son. He pulled the spike out of the swollen lump and a small drop of blood appeared where the spike had been.

'Brian, are you all right?'

'Yeah, I'm fine, Dad. It just stung a little. What the hell are those things?'

'I dunno son, but I think we should get out of here and get that looked at.' He looked at his finger, now swollen to twice its normal size.

Conor grabbed the oars off their cradles as he sat back in the middle of the boat.

'Dad they're still there.' Brian's voice was strained. 'And there's more now.' They could see ripples all around them.

'Don't worry son, we're leaving!' Conor started to

row, fast.

When he pushed the oars back, the oar on his right lifted one of those creatures out of the water. The creature – he didn't think of it as a fish any longer - didn't have any scales. It didn't have any fins on its smooth, spiked body either, even though it was shaped like a large salmon or trout.

Three of them stuck their heads out of the water and a line of spiky torpedoes followed them as Conor rowed. 'Down!' he shouted to Brian.

They dropped low enough so that the missiles shot over their heads. Conor grabbed the oars and put more power into each stroke.

'Why are they following us? What are they?' Brian asked. One side of his face felt immobilised, and his speech was a little slurred.

'I don't know son. I've never seen anything like them before.'

Something thumped against one side of the boat, and again on the other. Conor caught the look in Brian's eyes. 'It's okay; the boat is sturdy.' He could tell his words had little effect.

A row of spikes came flying through the air. Conor only saw them at the last second and pulled Brian to the floor of the boat while trying to get out of the way himself.

'Stay down.' He left Brian cowering and grabbed the oars again.

Any part of land would do now, and Conor started rowing toward the riverbank behind them.

Another thump hit the boat, louder this time, as the boat seemed to move again. Brian gave a little yelp and straightened up, staring at his father. Five spikes had connected with the left side of his head, two narrowly missed his eye.

'Pull them out, Brian! And stay down!' He kept rowing.

'Dad, there's one in your ear.'

'I know.'

Without thinking, Brian reached over to help his father when Conor saw another wave of darts flying toward them.

'Get down!' He pushed Brian down into the boat, and the spikes hit Conor full in the face. He felt the initial sting as they entered his skin. He had closed his eyes but one of the spikes connected with his eyelid and already he could feel it swelling along with the rest of his face.

'Brian, Brian, I can't see,' he said as his face sagged.

'Dad!' Brian started pulling the needles out.

'Don't worry about that now; just tell me where I'm going. We need to get off the river.' He reached for the oars, finding the left one but flailing about until he grabbed the right.

Brian looked at the bank behind them as his father started rowing towards it again. 'Yeah, that's it, Dad. Keep going.'

Three thumps banged off the boat, rocking it more heavily this time. 'Watch out for their spikes son, if they get you too we could end up going around in circles.'

'Just keep going Dad, we're nearly there.' Brian didn't tell him that they'd attacked again, although some spikes had landed in his father's arm.

Conor pulled harder. He could feel his muscles starting to ache and the oars getting heavier.

'Hurry, Dad,' Brian shouted. The creatures were swarming the boat, and for every ripple that went one way, two went the other. There were so many of those things now that the oars were connecting with them at each stroke.

'Come on, Dad. We're nearly there.'

Creatures rammed the boat, one after the other. The violent rocking made Conor drop the oars and hold on tight. Terrified, Brian grabbed hold of the edge of the boat as well. 'Keep going, Dad. Don't stop.'

Conor pulled with everything he had as a swarm of spikes came toward them. Brian ducked, but his father was hit in the face, arms and body. The swelling was instant and hindered his arms as he tried to row - they had become very heavy and sluggish. Brian could see they were only a few feet from the bank.

The boat slammed into the dirt wall and they fell forward. 'Get up Dad, hurry,' Brian said, getting to his feet.

The bank rose a few feet above the boat, and Brian helped his father to his feet while trying to keep the boat steady.

'You first, Brian.' Conor felt the grass beneath his

hand.

'No Dad, you go. I can see what I'm doing, you can't. Hurry!'

Conor didn't argue. He put his other hand on the bank and got ready to climb up onto the safety of land, reaching his hand back to find his son.

Suddenly the prow of the boat lifted up into the air, sending them tumbling backwards into the river. The force of them hitting the water was so incredible that they were swallowed instantly. An ice-cold blanket of immense pressure glued itself to their bodies and fought to keep hold. Brian was first to break through the surface of the water, gasping for breath, his arms splashing wildly. His father surfaced right behind him and struggled to stay above the water. Conor was a strong swimmer, but his numbed limbs were weighing him down.

'Dad ... help! Dad ... I can't stay afloat,' Brian shouted, spitting water out of his mouth.

'It's okay son, come to me.' Conor was terrified but knew he had to stay strong for his son.

'Dad, help!'

Conor moved in the direction of his son's voice and managed to grab hold of Brian's arm. 'I got you. Keep paddling.' Conor's arms were like lead, but there was no way he was going to let go of his son.

Brian did as he was told.

'Where's the bank?'

Brian looked around. 'Directly behind you.'

Suddenly Conor's legs were stung in multiple

places; those creatures had attacked again. His legs grew very heavy, very fast. 'Keep kicking Brian, harder,' his father urged, his legs nearly lifeless now. It was up to Brian to get them to the bank.

With the bank at his back, Conor turned around to reach up and grab hold of it. 'Climb up son, quickly!'

Brian pulled himself onto the grass with his father's help, then reached down and grabbed hold of his father's arm. Conor tried to pull himself up, but his arms and legs didn't have the strength.

'Come on, Dad!' Brian voice was full of terror as he tried to pull his father to safety.

Then, without warning, another wave of darts swarmed towards them. Brian had to let go of his father and cover his face with his arms. Conor was hit all over, above and below the water. His body tripling in weight as the poison sank in. He no longer had the strength to hold on, with the weight of his body dragging him down into the water. His fingers began to slip through the grass and toward the edge of the bank.

'I'm sorry, son,' he said, as his fingers lost their grip, slid off and he disappeared into the river.

'Dad! No!' Brian roared, reaching into empty space as his father's face was swallowed up by the dark waters. As he thought for a desperate moment of jumping in after his father, one of the creatures appeared on the surface of the water, then another, and another; within seconds they appeared to cover the whole surface. They stared at him, but made no attempt to attack. Brian knew this was a warning. They were telling him that the river was their domain now.

They dropped beneath the surface so fast that for a moment Brian wondered whether he had imagined the whole thing. But he hadn't. And he knew where they had gone. They went down to his father at the bottom of the river, leaving him on the bank alone, wet and fatherless.

They were doing the gutting today.

My Father's House
Sally Neary

It was strange saying goodbye to our mother. She had made the journey only once, when my eldest sister was an infant, and deemed it too far to repeat. Travelling with me was my sister Cathleen, my senior by fifteen years and in the way of big families, my second mother. I was nine years old and her proud co-pilot. I did not feel lonely leaving my mother for that first time. I was excited and so grown-up; I was in charge of my sister's cigarettes and could guess to the mile when the driver needed her next. My father had gone ahead of us. He had travelled to Dublin to his brother, Miceál, and they collected their sister from the airport and headed to their family home in south Kerry. This too was our destination. First we had to drive through the counties of Sligo, Mayo, Galway, Clare and Limerick keeping the Wild Atlantic Way to our right.

* * *

Back then, the Atlantic wildness remained unnamed and no one knew it had a 'way'. Living on the edge of this vast expanse of water we knew the next parish to Glencolmcille was America. The Atlantic was as familiar and unremarkable as the fresh air we breathed. Never referred to by its grand geographical title, it was just 'the bay'. Bunlacky was our favourite place, providing endless hours of enjoyment in summer. It was there we learned to swim, heeding my father's advice 'to walk out and swim in'. Unsupervised by adults, we'd jump and splash, urging others into the freezing water with calls of 'I've found a warm spot,' when secretly we'd peed in the water and found temporary relief from the cold.

The bay was also a magical place. The trawlers fished side by side, the growing winter dark making visible their lights that bobbed in Bruckless Bay. I was too young to understand that boats were electrically fitted, and to me they looked like they were carrying fire. My brother told me they were fairy lights. I liked to walk to the end of the Dunkineely town, where the sweep of the bay is revealed, to catch the magic of the sunset's glow on the remains of McSwine's Castle and be grateful that the fairies were content to remain in their watery home. We took for granted the sea's bounty: fresh crabs' toes, monkfish, cod and ling appeared on our table regularly. But the water was greedy, too. It demanded unfortunate souls who did not return from their week's work and were referred to as 'lost'. None of the fishermen learned to swim. It was thought that for those who fell into the sea it was better that you drown quickly rather than try to save yourself.

* * *

Having reached south Kerry, a county similar to Donegal in that it is surrounded on three sides by the Atlantic, we were tired and felt we had lost our way. The road had twisted and turned without any visible markings or signposts. It would have been easy to miss our final turnoff and end up in the Black Shop, a solitary, two-story building and the only shop-cum-pub for miles. Across its counter could pass creamy pints, sliced sides of bacon or fresh bread wrapped in tissue paper. The clientele would stand with their backs to the counter and push their caps off their foreheads, all the better to see us: two strangers with matching accents. That would be for later, for now we were intent on reaching our journey's end.

'This must be it,' I heard Cathleen say as she pointed the car to the left, off the narrowest of roads on to a bumpy track that curved towards a farm gate supported by two ancient pillars. Through it on the right, the orchard bounded the last bit of the lane. On the left sat a small green field, with space enough for young calves and shelter for the hens. The house sat proud, away from encroaching trees. Built by my grandfather, helped by my father and uncles, it had all the architectural simplicity of a child's drawing. The front door was flanked by two windows, and three upstairs windows sat beneath the eaves.

We abandoned the car by the side of the house. Aunt Kathleen came to meet us. With one arm held over her head to shield her eyes from the sun she grasped mine with the other. Her straight, grey hair was cut sensibly to her square chin, her eyes brimmed with emotion. She called to her brother Dan, small and kindly of face:

'They're here Dan. They're here.' And then I heard, 'Jim's daughters. Welcome.'

We are the daughters of her youngest brother, James, whom they always call Jim. The distance between Donegal and Kerry was so great they had never made the journey up to visit us and we had not travelled so far from home. When I was much older I was told that when my father had learned that his mother had died, either the journey was too long or costly for him, or the letter bearing the news of her death arrived too late, but he was unable to attend her funeral. This must have made her passing more difficult for him. It was our first time to meet our Kerry relations, though I grew up listening to stories about his native area. Everything was strange and so familiar.

'Welcome home.' Dan's soft voice said it all. I felt as if I had returned and yet how could this be? I was never further south than Dublin.

'Ye had a good journey?' my father enquired. 'Thank God to see ye here safe and sound.' He smiled, obviously pleased that having his children under his parents' roof for the first time with his own siblings closed a loop or completed one of his life's circles.

***

Dan and Aunt Kathleen remained single and continued living in the family home. The reason for our journey was to welcome their sister home from New York on holiday. She had left Ireland as plain Nellie Galvin and returned as Sister Ita, a Dominican nun who was only ever referred to by her name in religion. They were all very alike; physically strong, solid, well built. They also held definite opinions and were not shy in expressing them. At home in Donegal our father was the authority figure; not to be argued with, never to be interrupted. But here, with his own brothers and sisters, they questioned one another, waged verbal battles, wars of words which resolved themselves and dissolved into the ether. It was all in good fun. The respect and love in which they held each other was obvious. But one occasion put all that to the test.

***

We had spent the evening in the Black Shop, all with the exception of Uncle Dan and Aunt Kathleen. Pints of very black porter seemed to lubricate the conversation. Returning home, Sister Ita suggested we say the Rosary. No one protested. We were all kneeling on the cement floor that ran from the front door to the black stove in the kitchen. A single bulb lit up the kitchen and shone into the only other downstairs room, now darkened, the 'good room' with its covered circular table that was used as a dining area for us the visitors. Uncle Dan and Aunt Kathleen were more accustomed to eating at the stout wooden kitchen table beside the window, where sat the only connection to the outside world, their wireless.

My father was seated on the covered bench placed between the range and the stairs that opened up from the kitchen. Kneeling on the stairs I could smell the mothballs and camphor that wafted down from Aunt Kathleen's bedroom. Indeed the wooden partitions of all four bedrooms were no match for that strong aroma. Aunt Kathleen was a regular recipient of clothes parcels sent by Sister Ita from America but thought them too good to wear, so they were stored unworn in their mothball protectors, in a trunk at the base of her bed.

My father had bought a small quarter bottle of whiskey, his treat and antidote for the coming morning. On the third decade of the Rosary, Sorrowful Mysteries, the Crowning of Thorns to be precise, my father produced the bottle and handed it to Miceál, his senior by two years and his lifelong idol, inviting him to take a little sip. Without missing a Hail Mary or a 'glory be' he threw his head back and the whiskey disappeared down his throat. Receiving it back my father looked forlornly at the bottle.

'My best brother took the whole of my good whiskey.'

The Hail Marys, holy Marys continued but my father held his bottle tightly, staring into its emptiness as though it could reveal a mystery or relieve his disappointment.

***

I cannot remember any further prayers from my father that night. My sister and I giggled through the rest of the Rosary and to my amazement, got away with it. I began to see my father in a different light. He was no longer the remote, strict figure who lacked a lightness of touch. He had feet of clay.

I came to realise that for him it was a triumph of life to reach adulthood. He and his brother Miceál had survived the outbreak of the Great Flu of 1918. The family motto of 'Good food is better than good medicine' saw nearly all the family survive to old age. And what an age. His lifetime, 1900 to 1980, saw the death of empires and the birth of nations, too many lives lost in the process. Mr. Freud explored the psyche; Joyce rewrote our understanding of the English language; Picasso, art; Schoenberg and American jazz had changed music forever. My father had simply worked hard to ensure we ate well, keeping the kitchen stocked with the produce from his garden.

He was one the first gardaí of the Free State and although the pay was poor it all went on supporting and educating his growing brood of eight children. Maybe his character was formed by the very environment that bred him. Life on the western seaboard was not easy. Winters were and still are long and damp; houses were poorly built, medicine out the reach of most people and education basic. Perhaps it all contributed to a tenacious love of life, nation, faith and family. I have come to believe that our lives are as shaped and defined by our deep, wild and constant neighbour the Atlantic as any shoreline or indented coast. Walk through any town, village or townland on the west of Ireland and see the resultant determination and softness etched on every face.

On our return home to Donegal I did not tell our mother about the bottle incident. No, I was too busy regaling her with descriptions of the mountains, how they rose up from the coast and dominated the landscape. I told her stories of my father and Miceál coming home over the dangerous mountain pass, Coomakista, in the dark and fog. How too, in the absence of an indoor toilet it was best to make sure no one else had wandered past the linney, the outhouse store of home-grown onions and apples, on their way to what was referred to as a 'dry closet'.

I explained to my mother that it was possible to walk through the fields to the small bay, Bunowen, where my father had swam as a boy and where we swam, too. Did I tell her about the gentle peace that crept up the silent fields and settled all around the house and orchard? Probably not. But the story of the interrupted Rosary and the empty whiskey bottle did make its way into the family myth and legend, where it remains to this day. It has helped me come closer to the man who was my father. None of us are perfect. The acceptance of my father's imperfection gave me permission to accept my limitations as a parent. I have come to realise we do our best and trust that life will be kind to our weaknesses.

The Pheonix

Ann Garratt

I pull the handle of the front door and emerge from the dark interior into bright sunshine. People stream past me on the street, as if nothing has changed. Minutes later, as I arrive in the centre of town, a feast of summer bedding greets me - most striking are the orange and red begonias cascading from concrete tubs that soften the austere appearance of the Diamond.

I love it here, the honey-coloured stone of the ruined medieval castle looming in the background, the tall, brightly painted shop facades cradling the busy street and the pavements crowded with tourists. I stop for a moment and pull out my mobile.

'Just back from my check-up in Galway. Meet me in an hour for coffee, the usual place. I have something important to tell you both. Don't be late.' I'm waiting for my text to go when I realize I'm filled with apprehension. After everything that's happened, how will they react?

***

These past years have not been easy. The humiliation was the worst. My husband with my best friend's daughter. First the secrecy, then he left. Then he came back telling me it was all over with her. Then one day he said he couldn't live without her and he left again. The girls refused to forgive him and could never understand how their pensioner father could run off with a girl their age, but every time I looked in the mirror, I could. If it hadn't been for my daughters constantly reassuring me that I still had them, I don't know what I would have done. They say there's nothing like and old fool, and so it proved to be. He got his comeuppance in the end; she threw him out. He even tried to come back to me. But it was too late. My sympathy had long gone. I just wanted shut.

Soon afterwards I found the lump in my breast. For weeks I refused to believe it but when I told Megan, my youngest, that made it real. She accompanied me to the doctor. The rest happened so quickly I can hardly remember.

As it turned out the specialists in Galway were brilliant. I was lucky - they hoped they had caught it in time. But I never would have endured the gruelling weeks of chemo if it hadn't been for my lovely daughters. Their constancy willed me through it.

It's difficult to explain how it feels when you receive that diagnosis, but I can tell you that you feel violated and certainly scared. I remember Eileen, a young mother I met in the oncology unit. She was so determined to recover, to see her two boys grow up. We got to know each other when we were having chemo and kept in touch afterwards. She was so positive that everything seemed to be going well, but when she rang me six months ago I could hear in her voice what she did not have the heart to tell me.

We buried her last week.

***

And today, a year down the line, I'm still anxious whenever I attend a clinic. A couple of hours' drive to the appointment, the long wait for your turn to be called and then the news. The fear never leaves you. Just remembering it all makes my insides lurch.

I find myself outside my favourite shop and am thankful to be distracted by a sign in the window: Fifty per cent off. Well, it's worth a look inside. A few euros lighter I glance at my watch. Five minutes to go.

I am first at the café, so I sit down at a table outside and wait. There's a lovely breeze blowing and the smell of freshly baked bread is wafting my way, but my courage is deserting me. I leave my new purchase on the chair and head off to the ladies' to fix myself up. As I apply my lipstick, I glance in the mirror. Same face, same grey cropped hair, even my eyes look the same.

The girls still have not arrived and I feel a mounting panic. What will they say? Deep breaths. I try to rehearse the words but my mind's all jumbled. Rosie is first. She is smiling, but I can see she's worried behind that smile. Bless her, they've had so many summonses this past year. No wonder she's concerned.

Megan arrives a minute later and slumps down beside me. How could I be the mother of such stunners? They don't take after either of us, but have somehow managed to acquire the best features of both. Rosie has pale green eyes and dark hair like her father, and Megan has a mop of curly bright red hair like mine used to be, before it went grey. Now they look at me.

'What is it Mammy, what's wrong?'

'What did they say in Galway?'

I buy more time.

'Wait a minute I'll just order us a coffee. Then we can chat. Could you manage a scone?'

The girls shake their heads and I realise that I can't put it off any longer.

'Well, you know this has been a difficult time for me. What, with your father, then the cancer. It's been trying for us all. God knows how we've got through it. But we have. I am so proud of you both and we're all stronger for it. They say things happen for a reason, and I think it's to give us strength, to test us. But we have only one life to live and it's important we make the most of it.'

Megan butts in.

'Mammy what are you trying to say? You're worrying us. What is it? What's happened?'

I look from Megan to Rosie, gathering my

courage. I take a deep breath, put my leg up on the empty chair next to me and roll up my trouser.

The girls' mouths fall open.

I sit back in my seat, as both my daughters gape. Megan and Rosie look at each other, then burst out laughing. Their words spill out, almost giddy.

'You've had a tattoo?'

'Our sixty-five-year-old mother has a tattoo.'

'You're kidding.'

'It's a phoenix. I got the all-clear at the clinic this morning and thought what the hell. I had it done afterwards in Galway. Given the circumstances I thought it was very apt.'

My tattoo wasn't exactly subtle. The bird, with its bright red and orange plumage, soared from just above my ankle to half way up my calf. The flame of colour suddenly seems much brighter than it did in the tattoo studio earlier. But I love it.

'It feels so daring; I can hardly believe I've done it and it makes me feel twenty years younger. And that's not all. I've just bought the most delicious pair of cropped cream trousers to show it off.'

I pick up my coffee, take a sip and raise an eyebrow.

'What do you think?'

-THE END-

Wild Atlantic Words

MEAS Writers

MEAS Writers have been together since 2007 when they met during a creative writing class organised by MEAS and funded by the Donegal Vocational Education Committee, which is now the Donegal Education and Training Board (ETB). Our group is based in South Donegal and meets fortnightly.

Since its foundation, MEAS has organised multicultural poetry and prose readings at Donegal Castle (2010), the first time the Castle was opened for community use. MEAS storytelling and cultural events also took place at the Folk Village in Glencolmcille. The MEAS Writers most recent public event was an evening of music and stories at the Manhattan restaurant in Donegal Town.

Many of the asylum seekers and members of immigrant communities that MEAS has supported were introduced to the English language, Irish music, and education opportunities through the adult education programmes funded by the Donegal ETB and, importantly, the local Wild Atlantic people.

We have enjoyed our writing and have learned from each other. We hope our readers will enjoy these stories and perhaps feel tempted to pick up their own pen.

Darren Gallagher was born in County Donegal, where

he currently lives. Having dropped out of school at fourteen, he decided in 2008 to finally pluck up the courage and follow a dream that had been haunting him since childhood.

Receiving a diploma in creative writing from Kilroy's College in Dublin was the first step in re-learning the English that he'd forgotten, and that he never knew.

A natural night owl, when everyone else is sleeping, he hears the *bumps* and the *creaks*, captures them, and turns them into stories to make the hairs on the back of your neck stand up.

Darren is the author of *Strings*, *Love's Curse* and the forthcoming *Abyss*.

Ann Garratt was born in Ireland and at the age of seven moved to England, where she spent thirty-seven years before returning to County Donegal in 2006.

In 2010, Ann had five short pieces about her childhood broadcast on RTÉ Lyric FM and this provided the inspiration to begin her memoir, *The Road Taken*, which was published in 2014. She is a volunteer reporter for the Donegal Democrat and has had a number of her short stories published in Woman's Way magazine.

She is a keen gardener, enjoys walking and is an active member of her local book club. Ann lives in Donegal with her husband and a cat.

Charlie Garratt was born in Manchester, England and

fell in love with Donegal when he visited on holiday in the 1990s. He moved to Dunkineely in the south-western corner of the county in 2006 and started writing fiction shortly afterwards. His hobbies include growing vegetables, family history and playing the guitar badly.

Charlie won the Read LK short story prize in 2013 and his first novel, *A Shadowed Livery,* was published by Grey Cells Press in 2015. He is a member of the Crime Writers' Association and has been a member of MEAS Writers since it was established.

Marie Hannigan lives in the fishing port of Killybegs, County Donegal.

Two of her stories have won the Listowel Writers' Week short story award and she has written for radio and television. Spinning yarns or tall tales is a family tradition. The storyteller takes a few grains of truth and asks: *What if this happened instead of that? What if something else happened?* The reader may find a few grains of truth in her stories. The rest may be taken with a tablespoon of salt.

Sally Neary was born in Dunkineely, County Donegal. The youngest of eight, she studied at University College Dublin and Leicester University, UK. Sally started writing fiction only recently, but has spent a lifetime immersed in the love of books and listening to storytellers from her native area.

Sally has read her work on RTÉ's *Sunday*

Miscellany and at events throughout south Donegal, and regularly contributes to local press. A member of MEAS Writers for the past five years, she is deeply grateful for all their support and encouragement.

Clarrie Pringle blew in from Dublin years ago and has refused, despite many efforts, to be blown out of Donegal again, which provides all the craic needed to enjoy life.

Malachy Sweeney is the author of two books, *The Sands of Time* and *A Troubled Time*. His creative writing is influenced by a sense of place, a love of the sea and his interest in canoeing, sailing and fishing. In earlier years he worked on building sites in the north west of Ireland, Galway, Dublin and in England.

Malachy trained as a post-primary teacher and taught in Dublin before returning to his native Donegal, to teach at the Abbey Vocational School. In later years he was a director of the Donegal Community Chamber, and his nautical interest drew him to the Donegal Town Enterprise Scheme Ltd. (Donegal Bay Waterbus), where he served as chairman for a number of years.

Carolyn Farrar is a senior reporter with the Donegal Democrat and Donegal People's Press.

Born and raised in Queens, New York, her career in journalism has taken her on a series of ink-stained adventures with daily newspapers in Pennsylvania,

Washington, D.C., Connecticut and New York, as well as the occasional sojourn into radio.

Twenty years ago Carolyn arrived in west Donegal and traded the Empire State Building for Errigal. She is delighted to have worked with MEAS Writers as an editor on this anthology.

Wild Atlantic Words